I0595223

Hurst and Blackett

Jonathan Swift
Vol. I

ISBN/EAN: 9783337048136

Printed in Europe, USA, Canada, Australia, Japan

Cover: Foto ©Andreas Hilbeck / pixelio.de

More available books at **www.hansebooks**.com

IN THREE VOLUMES.

VOL. I.

LONDON:

HURST AND BLACKETT, PUBLISHERS,

13, GREAT MARLBOROUGH STREET.

1884.

Hurst and Blackett

Jonathan Swift

Vol. I

JONATHAN SWIFT.

CHAPTER I.

Mrs. Swift was free of the Brotherhood of Sorrow. The members of that fraternity do not cry for nothing. Few things preserve so rigid a loyalty to the rules of proportion as does real wretchedness. And so Mrs. Swift was half astonished to find herself sobbing over the letter on her knee—a simple note from Jonathan to say he was coming home— and fell involuntarily to wondering why she did it, and to looking back for explanation, in a dreamy way, as far as the black vista would let her.

What a mercy it is in the constitution of human nature that sorrow cannot be cumulative! Griefs cannot climb on each other's shoulders to pull us down. The latest black figure shuts out the view of the rest, holds them back, warns them off. Do you imagine that Job, when he heard of the strong wind that blew upon the corner of the house and knew himself childless, do you imagine that he thought then of his sheep and of his camels? Perhaps you do, reader; it depends on whether or not you have a soul. Mrs. Swift, at any rate, had not made *her* soul subservient to her reason, her divinity to her humanity, and she reaped the benefit just then. The chain of her retrospect snapped at a year before, broken by the chasm of a grave; and the shadows on the other side, where bitter poverty stood with his foot on comfort, and scorn had triumphed over respectful consideration, she scarcely saw. The memory of the father recalled the son.

Yes, it must be, he had failed again, was disappointed again, crushed again. The letter did not say so, but her instincts told her. Poor Jonathan! Nobody knows what it is to fail but those who deserve to succeed. But his mother knew *he* knew it. How bitter it would be, she thought. Twice! And worse than ordinary failure too. If he had not attempted more, he might have earned money. The wind howled outside, and Mrs. Swift shivered. She glanced at the tiny grate. The fire was out; on purpose, to save fuel. It need not have been, if Jonathan had hewn wood and drawn water—sacred wood and sacred water, because for his mother. And then she cried again; it was so bitter for him to know it.

She picked up his note and read it again. There was no hint as to when he would come, nor how; and the letter itself was dateless. Mrs. Swift thought a moment. The floods had made the roads scarcely passable for days, and if Jonathan had set off to walk from London, he could not be far behind his herald. With the inconsistency of love the mother's heart was cheered at once. It might be that night he would come. She listened. The rain was falling in torrents. How wet he would be should he come. The fire must be laid, at least, ready to light, and some tea put for him. His home-coming would not seem so bitter, if privation were kept out of sight just at first. So Mrs. Swift called,

'Lauriel, my pet, Lauriel.'

The door opened almost instantly, and Jonathan Swift's only sister entered.

'You called, mamma?'

'Your brother is coming home,' replied
Mrs. Swift, making an effort to put away
the thoughts of *why*, as they came crowding back, lest she should dash the happy
smile that had risen in the great lustrous
eyes which were gazing at her.

'Oh! I am so glad; won't it be nice,
mother mine,' said the girl, joyfully. 'He
must have sold his book, and is coming
back to write another. He shall give you
a new dress, mamma—that old thing is so
shabby—and he shall cheer you up, which
is ever so much better than all the clothes
in creation. Do you know, mamma,' the
girl ran on, 'I was stupid enough to be
frightened this morning because there was
no money left, and no dinner, no, not
enough for Towzer, in the house. Jonathan
made me promise before he went not to
adopt the Whig principle of getting into
debt, and, besides, I'm not at all sure our
credit is good enough to help me to break

my word if I would. Is he coming to-night, mamma?'

'I don't quite know,' answered Mrs. Swift; 'but you had better lay the fire, my pet, and put tea so that the poor boy can get it directly, if he do.' Away ran the girl with a rippling laugh. 'Lauriel,' called her mother, when she had reached the door, 'if your brother come, don't say anything about money matters—just at first. Jonathan will be tired. And, Lauriel, perhaps you had better say nothing even about his book.'

Half an hour later, Lauriel was survey-ing, with not altogether unmixed satisfac-tion, the result of her labours to brighten the dismal little chamber, when a footstep was heard outside.

'Surely, mamma,' she said, 'that is not Jonathan ! Those feet seem to sympathise with the ground they tread on, and I am sure *his* don't. No,' she continued, 'that is not his knock. That sounds like a sleepy artizan making day-wages ‚out of cold iron; not a bit like Jonathan, and Jonathan famous, too. Stay, mamma,' she cried, 'I will go.'

But Mrs. Swift had slipped past her and raised the latch. The dull tread was not so altered as to deceive *her*. Putting the door ajar, as though to look out, she whispered to her son, 'Let Lauriel be happy for to-night.' Then she kissed him.

The majority of men say that human beings have only five senses. A majority is generally wrong: and this is a case in point. Even the majority have more than five senses, they have more nearly fifty, or fifty times fifty. A sense is a means of communication with the mind and soul and spirit of a man, and if you tell me that all the impressions you remember to have felt came to you through your ears, or eyes, or nose, or taste, or feeling, I can only reply that nothing ever has made an impression on your soul and spirit. The operation has been confined to your brain. Oh! no; often does an influence come in upon the soul by one of those wicket-gates of heaven which we cannot see, nor define, nor predicate about, but only say we feel it is within us, and that its key is in the keeping of the God who made it.

His mother's kiss acted like a cordial on Jonathan Swift. He drew a long breath, and, without being aware of the effort he made, called out, in the cheeriest of voices,

'Well, mother, you are first: terribly well, I hope; and the little one, how is the little one?'

Lauriel dashed into his arms only to retreat again from the dripping figure with a silvery laugh.

'Go home, Neptune,' she cried, 'we haven't got a volcano to dry you at, and we don't want any seaweed, not to-day, thank you, not to-day.'

Then she stopped in amazement, and, staring at him, said,

'Might I ask, Mr. Neptune, whether it is with a view of getting all the salt washed out of you that you travel without an overcoat?'

Mrs. Swift trembled. There stood the great gawky body crowned by a face radiant, to all appearance, with happiness, in spite of the heart which moved its muscles being bruised almost to breaking. And Lauriel was close to him, gazing with an air of mock criticism straight into his eyes. He *must* wince under the unconscious thrust which reminded him that his ambition had only led to a pawn-shop.

'Such a long story,' he replied, pretending to look mysterious, ' *I put it into poetry as I came along.* You shall hear it presently.' Then he continued, 'Correspond to evaporation like a good little sun, as you are, and pull off my coat. Wo—o—Phaeton, take care, you'll sublime it if you're not careful.'

'Ah!' said Lauriel, 'what a mercy it is an old one, for it is quite spoiled.' It was the only one Jonathan Swift had left in the world.

'Nay, 'tis a beauty,' he laughed, as cheerily as ever. 'Now, I'm off to squeeze the rain out of my hair, for fear it should get through to the brain, and I'll be back in one moment to warm myself at the volcano.' Off he went.

Mrs. Swift lit the fire with a tinder-box, which seemed determined not to catch, it took her so long to strike a spark; while Lauriel, having vainly attempted to relieve her mother of the task, sat back in a chair and chattered away out of sheer happiness. The tinder caught, and the fire burnt up at last, however, in spite of Mrs. Swift's efforts, and she was obliged to face her daughter again with all the placidity her feelings would permit of. A very general effect sufficed fortunately ; one candle and a tiny fire are not good footlights; and even had Lauriel been predisposed to fancy anything was amiss and to scan her mother's face, the flickering shadow which rose and fell upon it, like the lapping tide of trouble, would have probably sufficed to conceal a little longer the bitter secret from detection, and have kept alive a little longer the happy laugh.

It is just possible, reader, that you do not see any rhyme or reason in this collusion between a brilliant man of genius and a respectable old lady to keep the knowledge of pauperism and ruin, and the anticipation of hunger, thirst, cold, misery, and wretchedness, from the sister of the one and the daughter of the other. If you do not, believe me, it is because you have no

conception what these things mean ; or because you never loved with that great love
which places another's happiness immeas-
urably above the desire for that other's
sympathy.

'What an age he is !' sighed Lauriel.
'Is he never coming ? I expect that story
of the great-coat is being put into poetry
now,

> " and Neptune coming will impart
> Impromptus he has learned by heart."

I've got a fit of the muses, mamma ; that's
because Jonathan has come home ; see how
they run—

> " The rising sun will scarce believe his sight
> Impromptus ! and yet ready for to-night !"

Listen, mamma,' laughed the girl, ' I am
certainly his sister, and his spirit pervades
the house.

> " Illustrious Neptune, listen, *we* hold
> Your wit is certainly your freehold.
> For you'ld be forced the pace t'increase
> If you held nothing but a lease."

I had better make the most of my time, hadn't I, mamma, and cap my own moral? Directly Jonathan comes I shall be as dull as—let me see—as usual.'

'I hope your brother is not ill,' said Mrs. Swift; 'he has been gone half an hour.'

And certainly Jonathan did not appear to be in any hurry. He was sitting in his room just exactly as he had gone to it, with his elbows on his knees and his chin resting on his hands, staring straight into a small mirror hanging on the wall. Shut your eyes, my friend, do not look over his shoulder, it is horrible. For he has looked so long that the image becomes real and looks back at him, and then he chuckles to it and edges his chair nearer to it, and it chuckles to him and edges its chair nearer to him. Then the chuckle dies away, and Jonathan Swift scowls awfully. Slowly, cautiously he lifts his nails, crooked, like vultures, to scratch the figure off the glass; but the eyes look in at him, and he dare not. Then, without uttering a sound, he raves at it, chatters with his teeth, jibes and jabbers and dances; but the unearthly eyes look at him still, and he feels their terror overcoming him. Back he slinks, and back and back, looking still because he must look, till, the corner reached, he crouches in it, palsied by the ghastly fear. He has sunk below the mirror, the spell is broken, and Jonathan Swift breaks out into a clammy sweat; for he knows he has been mad.

Just a moment for self-consciousness to re-assert itself, and he falls on his knees to pray with the fervour of despair for his mother, and Lauriel, and his ambition. He rose with such a feeling of extreme physical exhaustion as made it painful for him to stand upright; so, resigning himself for the moment, as he fancied, to the desire for rest, he lay down upon his bed, and was asleep in an instant, sound asleep. So sound indeed that Lauriel knocked again and again at the door, yet got no answer. She had come upstairs to see what had become of him. Oh, how he thanked God afterwards she had not come sooner! Then she partially opened the door and said, 'Jonathan.' No answer. Again 'Jonathan.' Still no answer. Then she went in and saw he was sleeping profoundly, just as he had arrived, soaked to the skin, his shirt-sleeves wet and his boots muddy; but his face was not the same, for the great forehead was ashy white, and the hard, drawn mouth did not look as if it could ever smile again. Then she saw it all; she could not but see it, and she would have liked to have left him and gone away and cried; but woman-like she remembered he was sleeping in his wet clothes at the risk of his life, so she went nearer to him and patted his cheek and said, ' Poor Neptune !'

Jonathan awoke with a start, drew his hand across his brow, and then, recollecting himself, he was going to force a smile, but Lauriel stopped him.

' Never mind, brother, it will all come right in the end ; you must win in the end, you know you must. Don't look like that,' she cried, ' don't look like that : you are going to let your heart break. Jonathan, Jonathan, remember mother !'

' Thank you, darling,' he said (and the look passed away), ' I will. I have been putting ambition before her and you ; it shall come last now. I will go to Moor Park to-morrow.'

CHAPTER II.

Moor Park was the residence of Sir William Temple. It was a great big house, and was kept up as a great big house, the capital of a large estate, ought to be. In the meantime, that is all I need say about it; for the jaded novel-reader will be thankful to learn that a description of the golden sheen of the setting sun and the landscape generally are not essential to an intelligent comprehension of Jonathan Swift's history. The only wonderful thing about Moor Park, it being a very large house indeed, was that Sir William Temple conveyed more honour to it by living in it than he got by owning it, which is very unusual indeed under the circumstances.

Most men are so much on a par of insignificance that the only way to distinguish them is by where they live. Nobody ever said, ' Sir William Temple of Moor Park;' one might as well have said, 'Adam of the Garden of Eden.' Perhaps this is not altogether a compliment to Sir William. It is almost equivalent to saying that he was not a man of the highest order by any manner of means. Genius very rarely indeed succeeds in filtrating through stratum after stratum of minds down to the common herd in the course of a lifetime, unless that be a very long one ; and when a statesman at fifty is perfectly understood and appreciated, it is because his stock in trade is talent, which, being thin, drains quickly. This was distinctly true in the case in point. No one could accuse Sir William of genius—it would have been as sane to accuse him of manslaughter; yet he was very clever indeed, a brilliant scholar, a clear-headed, shrewd man of business, an acute negotiator, and, as follows, of course, a successful statesman. Which means he had ordinary parts, great diligence, and a most retentive memory. Jonathan Swift said bitterly, when, one day in after years, some friends were commenting on Sir William's enormous power of recollection—'Time! what of it? He ought to be able to remember everything through eternity, for his memory is his soul.'

Sir William Temple was a distant relative of Mrs. Swift's. He was a cousin four times removed—twice by blood, once by his reputation, and once by Moor Park; nevertheless, he was the nearest relation Mrs. Swift had left, and the one to whom she would be obliged to apply for assistance if the worst came to the worst; unless, on consideration, she preferred to starve. Jonathan had seen the great man once, two years before, and, as the result of this interview, had registered a solemn vow never to see him again till all the obligation of mutual intercourse should be on the other side. He had asked for assistance, and had been offered charity. What an enormous difference there is between the two! The one is emancipating a man and the other buying a slave. And Jonathan Swift had refused the offer. Twenty-three is hopeful, conscious strength is hopeful, and unless one faces despair it seems hard to let one's best feelings gorge the appetite of pride. Two years had made a difference, however, in his point of view. Twenty-five was not quite so sanguine; for the moment it was not sanguine at all—and the conscious strength! Oh, those two minutes by the mirror!

Accordingly, when Jonathan Swift said,

at the close of the last chapter, that he would go to Moor Park, he meant it, in defiance of his vow; and when, ten minutes later, he walked slowly downstairs to join his mother and sister in the sitting-room, he had quite made up his mind. He sat down by the fire and tried to forget the awful experience he had had upstairs. No, nothing would ever help him to do that, but ' Itself.' He shuddered.

' You are cold still, Jonathan,' said Mrs. Swift. ' Drink this brandy, and don't trouble to talk to-night. To-morrow, when you are rested, will be time enough.'

It was a relief to talk, however, and so he answered by saying,

' I went to see Windmarsh among others, and as to the rest, I need not trouble you. Those men are all cut from one pattern—a brown-paper one, you know—and the consequence is that they have a desperate partiality for the rags

which helped to make them; to such an
extent, in fact, that they won't be decently
civil to any other rags. It certainly is
not marvellous that they are so slow in
estimating brains, for they are, beyond
all question, shrewd enough in judging
of appearances, and what old clothesman
or fashionable tailor ever was a judge of
Homer or Milton? Yes, for a sample, you
may take my reception from Windmarsh.
I went to his shop and asked to see him.
What was my business? asked the clerk,
quite unnecessarily; he knew the formula
as well as though I had gone through it
the day before. A book to sell? Ah, yes,
would I wait? So I waited an hour and
a quarter, until Windmarsh came out of
his den to see me. I saw that he had
taken-in all my separable attributes at
a glance; and at a glance I saw that
he never would, or could, take-in my

inseparable attributes. Clothes were his vocation distinctly, when men were concerned, and binding, when books. "Are you the man who had the suicide on Snow Hill to describe for me?" he asked. But I assured him I was not, and presumed to roughly indicate the wares I had for disposal. It was the "Tale of a Tub" that I had with me. He picked it up and glanced over it. Oh, how his lip curled! How he despised it! Presently he chanced on that part where it is described how the three brothers find in their father's will their justification, *totidem literis*, for wearing shoulder-knots. I always thought that piece would make the fortune of the book; and so it will, because Windmarsh did *not* think so. Indeed, when he came to it, he read it out, looked me straight in the face, and asked me whether I really thought such ridicul-

ous rubbish was wit, and whether any
sane man would laugh at it except in
derision ?'

'Oh, Jonathan,' said Lauriel, 'I hope
you snubbed him well.'

'No,' answered her brother, 'I was
toady enough to refrain ; but remember,
I was cold, hungry, and penniless. And,
besides, there was no use in my trying
to be quits with him ; for, though he
could give me money, I certainly could
never give him brains.'

'Did they all think equally bad of your
work, Jonathan ?' put in his mother.

He got up and walked backwards and
forwards across the little room before he
answered. It requires some moral courage to confess absolute failure, even to
those who are nearest and most sympathetic, and even when we have only failed
in the eyes of so many Windmarshes.
Then he said, 'Yes,' and, forcing a laugh,

added, 'It may fairly be said that I have failed utterly. No one would take the "Tale of a Tub" at a gift.' There was more implied in what he said than he cared to express just then.

'What models of wisdom!' said Lauriel, bitterly.

'In good sooth they are,' replied her brother. 'And they are very generally copied. Oh, they have a large following in their wit!'

'It will come all right some day, Jonathan,' said Mrs. Swift, striving to be, cheerful.

'Ah! yes,' he answered, 'so I believe, and have written on that ground a dedication to "Prince Posterity;" but you see, mother, we can't wait to be fed by that illustrious individual. You and Lauriel must have bread, and a roof to cover you; and all the recognition coming centuries may lavish upon me won't give you those:

not a crust, not a tile!　No, I have failed in earning money by my brains, and that was what I wanted to· do.　The fame would have come in good time.　One of the half-dozen men capable of appreciating it would have come across my book some day or other, and then, when bidden by a Somers, the mob would have cheered to the skies.　But it was money I wanted; it was a question of self-preservation with me; I wished to earn a living, that was all, and the inner circle of the world I would appeal to, refused the author of the " Tale of a Tub " his dinner.'

'Perhaps,' he added, wearily, while the ever-present thought of those terrible moments surged black upon him, 'perhaps I am wrong.　Windmarsh may be right— the " Tale " may be all nonsense.　You see it is the second trial and the second book. I have wasted two years on the venture, was I wrong after all?　Have I no more brains than Saul and his brethren and his father's asses?   Well, be it so, just now. I will try no more—just now.   There is no time for experiments. Something must be done to buy you a new dress, mother,' he went on, unconsciously quoting Lauriel's happy words of so short a time before, ' and to put some coals on the fire. To-morrow I intend to do it.'

There was a long, sad silence in the dis-mal little room.   Jonathan Swift's resolve looked like the grave of so many hopes no one of those three mourners had ever dreamed of burying out of his sight, that it was very, very bitter. Presently Lauriel got up and went to where he sat, thinking, thinking, thinking, in spite of himself, of ' *It*,' and wondering whether It was coming back again.

' Jonathan,' she whispered, ' you won't be angry with me, will you, if I propose something you don't like ?   I am sure it is a very good idea, and quite feasible too. There is nothing against it, indeed there isn't, and you could go on writing just until you happened to hit on some popular notion which might take, and induce everybody to run after your better pieces, and then there would be fame, and money, and everything. You will consider it, Jonathan, won't you, before you quite make up your mind?'

'I fear, Lauriel pet,' he answered, 'the case is beyond your magic; what is the treasure-trove, sweet seventeen, that will work such wonders?'

'Promise first, Jonathan, you won't be angry.'

'Not unless you are very naughty indeed,' he replied, with a sad smile. Then he picked up one of her hands that rested on his knee, while she leant over him, and was going to kiss it. 'Lauriel,' he said, 'what have you been doing with your hands? They are not so delicate as they used to be; and, now I think of it, where is Mary? I have not seen her all the evening. You brought in tea yourself.'

'Oh, Jonathan,' she answered, 'she was so much trouble, far more trouble than she was worth, really we get on much better without her, really we do, and, Jonathan, (mind you have promised),' she went on, dashing at it, 'I have been amusing myself by doing up a few Steinkirks and cuffs for the people at Herne Castle. They think I do them very nicely, they do indeed, Jonathan, and I could get lots more to do from round about, and make plenty of money to live here, it costs very little, and you could write till the time came, it couldn't be long, Jonathan, when the world would find you out, and honour you. Do, please, let me do it, do, please!'

There was a pause, and Jonathan Swift caught himself guessing curiously whether the demon of failure had any lower depths to lead him to than this; then he answered, in a voice so unnaturally devoid of animation, that Lauriel started, and for the instant doubted whether it were her brother who had spoken,

'Ah! let me see, you are to be a washer-woman, and I am to live on your earnings, say for ten years, say for twenty. Oh! Lauriel, how could you——?' Then, clasping her in his arms with unusual passion, 'Unselfish little angel, no, no, no! I tell you, Lauriel, I had rather fail for ever.'

CHAPTER III.

THOUGH Jonathan Swift stuck to the spirit of his determination, he was obliged to modify its letter. Things had come to such a pass at the cottage, and the deficiency in ways and means was so complete, that it was absolutely necessary for him to make some arrangement which should tide his mother and sister over the short time which would elapse before they could receive the charitable dole his proud spirit had steeled itself to beg from the distant cousin. So he spent next day in making promises to the landlord and praying for consideration from the butcher and baker;

and he was surprised to find how easily his promises were accepted and his prayers agreed to.

'Sir,' however remarked the last tradesman he visited, 'Mrs. Swift has always paid cash until now; and besides, if you will pardon my saying so, Miss Lauriel is bound to marry a duke some day—that is, sir, if dukes have tastes in keeping with their position.'

Jonathan was enlightened by this speech in a way he did not at all appreciate. It was a signal flash from a rock ahead which until now he had forgotten or ignored. If Lauriel was so glaringly pretty that a butcher could see it with his naked eye, taking care of her became a very serious responsibility. She must evidently be perfect; for Jonathan knew she was pretty, and nothing appeals equally to a butcher and a poet but the unquestionable. So the brother began to cast over anxiously in his mind every possible person within a radius of ten miles who might take it into his head to marry Lauriel, and was rejoiced to find the number exceedingly small. At the same time he made a mental resolution that the married baker should certainly wait for ever for a settlement of his bill rather than that the bachelor butcher should be their creditor for a penny. He shuddered to imagine his sister obtaining his discharge from a debtor's prison by accepting as her lord and master this slayer of beeves or another like him.

Gentle reader, Jonathan Swift was not a snob. Permit me incidentally to explain the word. A snob is an individual who attempts, successfully or otherwise, to obtain a character he does not deserve. Eating peas with one's knife is not snobbish; it is boorish. Pray pardon this lecture *à la* Trench; but the word is so very generally misapplied that, without the explanation, most people would have imagined, when they read that Jonathan Swift was not a snob, that he was a man with whose political convictions they had every sympathy. No, he was not a snob. He had no objection to a butcher as such. That is to say, he did not pretend to be a higher and more perfect representative of his genus than a butcher *might* be. All he did pretend was to be a higher and more perfect representative of his race than the butchers he had chanced to encounter, and of whom he had heard, were. So far as his experience extended, he did not believe that the slaughter-house was peculiarly calculated to develop the higher nature of those who spent their time there. That was all. But it was enough to make him very anxious about leaving his sister in the false position of being the equal or inferior of such people in the eyes of the world. However, there was no help for it, and he only determined to warn his mother seriously to beware of everybody, from the butcher's duke to the duke's butcher.

It was dusk when Jonathan reached home, and the rain, which during the day had allowed the soaking earth a short respite, began to fall afresh. The wind rose with startling rapidity. Lurid clouds gathered densely, far as the eye could reach, and presently the lightning began to flash and the thunder to rattle. Lauriel opened the door.

'How awful it looks!' she said. 'Come in, Jonathan, come in.'

He looked at her as she stood in the porch, with the dull, unnatural light upon her face reflected from the metallic-like clouds, while, with frightened eyes and clasped hands, she shrank from the artillery of heaven. She was surpassingly beautiful, but he saw she was part of a picture. Those clouds—were they ominous? And then he smiled again, for he remembered he stood between her and them. Rash self-confidence of genius, fate smiled back.

That evening, as the three sat dismally enough listening to the raging hurricane crashing madly among the trees, there came a knock at the door. It was repeated again and again, uselessly, for the noise of the tempest disdained that any meaner sound should be audible. Presently a lull came, however, and then the loud rapping penetrated to the sitting-room. Lauriel went at once to the door, and had scarcely opened it when a manly voice called out,

'Well, young woman, I suppose I can come in out of the weather?'

Jonathan was close behind his sister, having risen just after her.

'Yes,' he said, 'pray come in, *for* it is not a night when we can turn a dog out of doors.' He did not at all like Lauriel being spoken to in that exceedingly familiar way by any stray wayfarer, so he accentuated the 'for.' It served his purpose.

Henry, Count de Guiscard, was of the number of those who understand inflections, and it was he who had been lost in the storm and had addressed Lauriel as 'young woman.' Seeing at a glance that he had not got ordinary ten-pound householders to do with, he modulated his tone accordingly.

'I beg ten thousand pardons,' he said, bowing profoundly; 'but really, upon my honour, the wind has nearly blinded me.'

A terrific crash, as a gust tore a limb from a tree and hurled it to the ground, drowned the rest of the apology.

'Pray come in,' repeated Jonathan,

pacifically, as in duty bound, though something jarred upon him in an indefinable way, and made him dislike the tall stranger in spite of his polite tact.

So the Count de Guiscard went in and proceeded to pay for his entertainment by being as agreeable as he could, speculating in the intervals as to where on earth he was, and who these refined, highly cultivated people were, to whom, nevertheless, the difference between a penny and three-halfpence was plainly of great consequence.

'I lost myself utterly,' he laughed, 'and hardly expect to know where I am ever again in the world.'

Jonathan took the hint.

'My name is Swift,' he said. 'Allow me to introduce you to my mother and sister; we are here about two miles due west of Merton.'

The count bowed.

'My name is Guiscard,' he said; 'it

would be egotistical to tell you who I am, because it would monopolise the conversation of the evening. People get partly over the difficulty by calling me a soldier of fortune; but that is distinctly incorrect, because she fights against me. I have got the better of her to-night,' he added, cheerily, 'and have to thank you for the kind co-operation which has enabled me to take her in flank.'

Good spirits are contagious. Jonathan began to be less gloomy.

'Soldiers have an enormous advantage over the rest of mankind,' he said; 'fortune can't avoid being either on one side or the other, and the side on which she isn't need not wait; whereas ordinary mortals, not being certain of where she is, have no notion of which point of the compass to betake themselves from or to.'

'Ah !' said the count, 'that would be all very well if there were no soldiers but soldiers; but you forget the Commissariat Department. Fortune is horribly exhausted in the victualling.'

Lauriel laughed.

'Don't you think,' said the count, appealing to her, 'don't you think it very hard that in time of war the enemy should destroy us, and in time of peace the civilians disband us; that the foe should gloriously knock us on the head if they can, and the friend gloriously starve us to death if they can't?'

'Oh!' she answered, 'death and no pay is so much worse than life and half-pay that I think the government do all that can be expected of them. It would be a hardship to the slain if the warriors who survive them were to get still more than they do out of their continued existence.'

> ' " Who draws his sword and runs away
> Continues still to draw his pay,
> But who upon the field lies slain
> Will draw nor sword nor pay again," '

said Jonathan, rhyming as he needs must when occasion offered.

'I surrender at discretion,' laughed Monsieur de Guiscard. 'Defend myself I cannot, and run away I cannot (in spite of your recommendation), because you are so ready with your "feet." Tell me,' he added—'I appeal to you as a poet—is the ascent of Parnassus a penance or a practice; does one climb to learn the goose-step, or because one *has* learnt the goose-step?'

'I protest against your answering that question, Jonathan,' said Lauriel. 'Unless you wish to spend the rest of your natural life in listening to a dissertation on the nature and essence of poetry, do please, Monsieur Guiscard, withdraw the interrogatory.' She hesitated a little before saying, 'Monsieur.'

The count spoke English with complete fluency, and without any trace of foreign construction in his sentences; but his accent here and there bore marks of an alien tongue.

'You are right,' he said, pleasantly, 'I am as French as French can be. I have lived days and days and days without tasting roast beef—once a whole fortnight, but that was during a state of siege. I have laughed dozens of times for the pleasure of the thing, and without entering the occurrence in a note-book; I wrote the epitaph of my best friend in a ball-room.'

'Oh, fye!' said Lauriel.

'It was my own,' went on the count. 'I——'

'A thousand pardons,' interrupted Jonathan; 'do be so good as to quote the epitaph.'

'No, and again no!' laughed he. 'It is bad enough to read an epitaph after one's death, when one is forgotten. But the contrast with the living subject—I couldn't be submitted to it; not yet—no, not yet.'

'There is one in the neighbouring churchyard,' said Jonathan (stretching his imagination for the occasion), 'which describes in an inimitably succinct manner the diverse qualities of piety and humour which the remembered dead was possessed of—

" Hic Jacet John Thompson escaped from life's yoke,
' I will meet you above,' were the last words he spoke.
Ah! he *was* such a fellow to crack a good joke!" '

'They have done Mr. Thompson grievous wrong, one way or other, surely,' said the count, ' he couldn't think life a " yoke," and he couldn't leave it in the sense of escaping from it, if he really had any sense of the ridiculous. This I'm quite sure of, that though he might find the world he went to a great deal better than this one, he wouldn't find it half as funny. One doesn't laugh when one is happy, one laughs when one is amused. There can't be anything amusing there, there can't be anything to laugh at. There can't be anything flippant. Oh! dear me, I am much afraid heaven was not made for Frenchmen.'

'Or, monsieur,' said Lauriel, with a tinge of seriousness underlying her tone of banter which did not escape Monsieur de Guiscard, 'is it *vice versâ ?*'

'Very possibly that is so,' he replied; 'but you must admit that either way is hard, very hard.'

'Really,' said Jonathan, 'it seems to me that nothing completely satisfies you either as regards things present or things to come; for you have scarcely finished abusing this world with half-pay in the bargain, before you come knuckles down on eternal felicity as being deficient in humour.'

' As you are stout, be merciful,' laughed De Guiscard, ' or stay, I shall beat a retreat and save my character for infallibility (at least in my own eyes) before you have time to destroy it utterly. How late it is,' he continued, looking at his watch, ' I fear I have kept you all up, thoughtlessly, far beyond regulation hours.'

' We have to thank you for brightening up our evening wonderfully,' said Jonathan.

' Indeed you have,' added Lauriel.

' All the obligation is on my side,' answered De Guiscard, ' and I have enjoyed myself'—he hesitated—' beyond expression, and that is a very great deal, you know, or it would not surpass my chatter. Pray make my excuses to madame, your mother.' (Mrs. Swift had quietly slipped away some time before.) Then he went off to his room, Jonathan leading the way, but first he shook hands with Lauriel, and put just a suspicion of adoration into the clasp.

CHAPTER IV.

THE Count de Guiscard rose early next morning, very early indeed. He had not slept much; the storm did not admit of it; and besides that he recognised, with the eye of a man accustomed to face emergencies, and to conquer them too, that if the idea, come to him on the wings of the tempest, were to bear him fruit it must strike its roots at once. So he cultivated it assiduously all night as he lay and listened to the howling of the wind, and when morning dawned he went to satisfy himself as to the only remaining unknown quantity in his calculation by consulting his mirror.

‘That will do,’ he sighed to himself, as he looked. ‘I am very reasonably good-looking and exceedingly like a gentleman; yes, that will do.’

Monsieur de Guiscard had often satisfied himself about this fact before. That was precisely why he did it again. It rather surprised him that, at last, he had not begun to look like—himself. Presently he went downstairs. Lauriel was sweeping the sitting-room. He slipped past, opened the front door, stood in the porch and waited. It was just possible that Lauriel might not like their poverty exposed so clearly to a stranger, and would be pleased at his tact in being pointedly blind to it. In a minute or two she came to the door, however, broom in hand.

‘I think this letter is yours, Monsieur

de Guiscard,' she said, and added, with a smile, 'It was considerate of you not to frighten us last night with your title, but you see my crest is more illustrious than yours—*planta genista!*' and she showed her broom in a pretty mock triumph.

Evidently it did not occur to her to be ashamed of her insignia of office.

'Pardon me for remarking,' he replied, a little gravely, 'that I don't think that *is* your crest.'

There was a tone of kindly sympathy in his voice that touched Lauriel. Ever since the necessity had arisen, she had done the work of charwoman without a murmur, even to herself. But it was very hard, nevertheless, to one trained as she had been, and with a temperament such as she possessed. So she felt thankful to Monsieur de Guiscard for his insinuation that her chief end was not sweeping floors or cooking dinners.

'How quiet the morning seems to be by contrast with last night,' she said, for the sake of changing the subject.

'Don't you think the morning always does?' he answered, turning round and facing her fully. 'Or no, you will not, but to me it does; let me tell you why. It is as good a peg to hang what I have to say to you upon as any other. A drowning man makes slight distinctions between the straws he clutches at. Miss Swift, I am being 'hunted—to death.' She turned very pale. 'Look,' he continued, half-drawing his sword, that showed a dull, red blue upon its blade. 'Look.'

She shuddered and drew back.

'Murder!' she gasped.

'If that is a synonym for self-defence against a peer of the realm, when the assailed is only a French count, yes!'

'Who was it? When did it happen? Where?' she asked, with difficulty fighting against her terror.

'Pray do not be alarmed,' he answered, in a tone of gentle sadness that reassured her—surely no vulgar cut-throat could speak like that. 'It is unutterably selfish of me to frighten you thus, simply for the sake of saving my insignificant life; but there is more than that at stake,—my honour. Oh, I cannot bear to die the death and leave the reputation behind me of a felon, because of a crime I have not committed, a deed I have not done. Listen, Miss Swift, I have only been aware of your existence for a few hours. My mind was made up to this, when I had been aware of it for a few moments. My life, my honour, are absolutely in your hands—that is the first thing. And now I will tell you why I presume to ask for your protection, and why I think you will accord it to me.

'I served last year in Germany as captain in a French infantry regiment, a regi

ment somewhat celebrated for its luck in
always seeing a good deal of the enemy.
As a consequence of its fame in this
respect, a very considerable number of
young bloods, who wished to win a character for courage, used, at the opening
of every campaign, to join the ranks as
volunteers, see us through a big battle,
and then go home with their laurels.
Well, it chanced, as the malignancy of
fate would have it, that among these there
appeared last year a younger brother of
Lord Mohun. He chose my company,
and joined it whilst I was away on a
few days leave of absence, and was a very
disagreeable surprise to me on my return.
I disliked him instinctively; he hated me.

'Before very long he backed ingloriously
out of a wine-shop squabble with some
civilians, and, for the credit of the regiment, I was forced to report the matter
to our colonel. The affair was hushed

up, however, the authorities having received general orders from home to be most careful not to offend influential foreigners who might be some day of use, and especially to let the young Englishmen of family do as nearly as might be just what they pleased. Nevertheless, I had made an enemy who was vindictive in an inverse ratio to his want of courage, and against whom I could scarcely hope to defend myself in the long run, joining as he did great influence to his hatred, and wealth to his implacability. Of course I had friends, but they were mere gentlemen and officers like myself, and as for money, I was dependent (with the exception of a few hundreds a year) entirely on my commission. I took the only course open to me under the circumstances, and challenged him to fight. He evaded the challenge by obtaining an order sending him instantly to the front with some despatches.

' At that time the enemy were believed to be retiring before our advance, and to be beyond striking distance. The Hon. Ernest Fitzjames (that was his name) had not long started on his mission, however, when couriers announced that the foe were massing in great force, evidently determined to fight, and that reinforcements were urgently required to sustain our advanced position in case of an attack. My regiment, among others, was at once ordered off, and by dint of a forced march of twenty miles on a stormy night we arrived just as the expected action began. The necessity was so great that we were obliged to dash straight at the enemy without even snatching a moment's rest.

' What was my astonishment, as I scrambled across a ditch which lay in our road, to find in its safe shelter, well hidden by weeds, mud, and stagnant water, the *Hon.* Mr. Fitzjames. My men were dead tired, the least check would have damped their ardour; to have seen me stop for an instant would have meant the retreat of my company, and it might very possibly not have stopped there; so, without waiting even to put this pink of chivalry under arrest, I leapt the hedge and rushed straight forward. As luck would have it, the impetuosity of our attack saved us from having to repeat it, and the enemy retired sullenly to his entrenchments.

'The instant I could be spared I ran back to the ditch in hopes to find my man still among the rushes. But no, he had gone. I was surprised at this, for the roar of the artillery had hardly ceased, though the muskets had been silent for some time, and I did not fancy he would stir from his refuge until not a shot menaced his valuable existence. Had he recognised me as I charged over him, and been more terrified to remain than to fly?

'When this thought struck me, I emerged from the ditch, intending to relinquish my search, and looking a good deal dirtier than the stains of legitimate battle and march had made me. Imagine my astonishment when a guard of ten men, headed by himself, suddenly surrounded and arrested me on the charge of having been guilty of gross cowardice in forsaking my company when ordered to charge, and hiding in that ditch. The effrontery of the thing paralysed me. I surrendered my sword as in a dream, and was marched straight off to a drumhead court-martial.

'On the way it occurred to me that I should have great difficulty in proving my innocence. It is wonderful how little one sees during a battle except what is straight before one. It was quite possible that not a man in my company would be able to swear to whom it was that led the charge.

They would only see some one in a certain uniform waving a sword. I was reassured by reflecting, however, that the lieutenants' uniforms were so different from mine that the men would be sure to know a captain was present; besides which, only one lieutenant went into action in my company, the other being wounded and in hospital.

'There was little time for doubt. A court was constituted on the spot, and then—think of it—*he* swore to having seen me hide, to having taken command of the company when the lieutenant was shot—as he had been, poor fellow, early in the action—and to having returned to arrest me when all was over. You must remember that the volunteers of rank wore a uniform closely resembling that of a captain in the regiment in which they chose to serve. Indeed the only difference was in the epaulets.

'I told my story. My men were questioned; but, with the exception of an old sergeant, who was positive he had seen my face as I cut down a gunner by one of the guns we captured, no one was sure whether I had been myself or somebody else. Several, however, had seen the incident in point, and knew the captain, whoever he was, had sabred a gunner, and it fortunately occurred to the President to look at both my sword and that of my accuser. Mine was bloody, his was clean. I was released. The Hon. Ernest Fitzjames asserting very justly that finding me innocent was finding him guilty, left the regiment and returned to England.

'I fancied I was saved. But no. In a few weeks an order came from court to dismiss me from the army, as "it was incredible that Mr. Fitzjames should be guilty of gratuitous falsehood." Orders were further given to spare my life as a reward for past services!

'From that moment I devoted myself to the sacred task of clearing my tarnished honour from the stain it bore. With this view I came to England and dogged my enemy's footsteps. I wished to meet him in the presence of two men of undoubted probity, and force him with my sword to tell the truth before them. I could never accomplish it. Often I could have killed him when alone, but that would have been worse than useless.

'One day he came unexpectedly into a tavern where I sat alone. I shall never forget his face as it looked when he recognised me. I slowly rose and cursed him under my breath, but did not offer to draw. That he saw, and guessing why, knowing he was safe as yet, he smiled. Oh! God, he smiled, a hideous, satanic smile of delight at my misery, and then went quickly away. It was useless waiting longer; he had seen me, and would be very careful for some time to come—besides, it was unsafe. Means would be found to remove me.

' So I left London, meaning to hide somewhere till my foe was lulled again. Now listen. Last evening at dusk, 1 should think forty miles from this, three desperadoes, having the *Honourable* man at a safe distance behind them, set upon me when tired and alone. I felt half inclined to let them do their worst; but the recollection that I should die dishonoured nerved me. It was foolish to kill them, for I did not doubt the arch-fiend in the rear had some story ready which would hang me for it, so I tried to escape by fairly running away. One poor wretch, however, was too fleet of foot, and—I was forced to——

' Then I ran again, ran, ran, ran for six hours by byeways, woods, and meadows, absolutely as fast as I could, away from

injustice, the gallows, irretrievable dis-
honour, everlasting reproach, till, utterly
worn out by fatigue and the tempest, I
reached this—is it to be a haven?'

His voice trembled a little, and his
handsome eyes were clouded by a look
of weary sadness. Lauriel was deeply
touched.

'What can we do for you?' she asked,
simply. 'How hard it is!'

'You can let me stay here,' he answered. 'It is far from the scene of *this*,'
touching his sword significantly; 'no one
unacquainted with the speed of foot and
endurance I possess would believe it possible I could yet be so far from it. Besides,
this is the very last place they will think
of looking for me in. What interest could
you have in abetting my concealment?
Nobody will dream of such a thing. No,
here I am safe; elsewhere I am lost—I am
lost.'

'You shall stay. You shall be saved, if we can do it. Jonathan is clever, he will do it if it can be done. Oh, how wicked the world is! Tell me,' she cried, passionately, as all the wrongs and troubles of those nearest and dearest to her seemed to shine out more clearly than ever in the glare of this great iniquity, 'tell me is it all bad, wicked, dishonest, hateful? Is there nothing that is good?'

'Yes,' he answered, with a bitter smile, 'there is—the ideal.' Then, changing his tone, he went on, rapidly, 'Pardon me, Miss Swift, but you must not tell your brother, nor your mother, yet. The house is liable to be searched at any moment, and, if they know I am still here, they will either have to betray me or—which would be worse—tell a lie, and, even if they did tell a lie to save me, they could not tell it well enough to serve the turn. Ah! Miss Swift, few people can help telling the truth most significantly when they fancy they are misleading most. Besides, there is risk in this: none for you, you are a girl, not one would have the heart to punish you for an act of Christian charity. But your brother? It might be very serious indeed for your brother to know. In fact, I would not for worlds be guilty of allowing him to run any such fearful risk as would thereby be incurred, for a stranger and an outcast like myself. No; I would rather face my fate at once with my conscience clear and only pray to be forgotten.'

'Jonathan is going away to-day,' she said, her eyes filling. 'Poor Jonathan!'

Monsieur the Count de Guiscard drew a long breath. His well-drilled features nearly broke away from control, and a smile was so imminent that he was forced to clasp his brow with his hand, as though in a dull effort to stroke away the care

that sat there.   This news simplified matters so very much from the count's point
of view, as the reader will see immediately, that his satisfaction is scarcely to be
wondered at.

'It shall be as you wish,' said Lauriel,
looking at him with a great pity.

Then he recovered himself, and, taking
her hand reverently in his, said, with
solemn emphasis,

'May the God of the merciful bless
you.'

CHAPTER V.

Jonathan Swift was nearing Moor Park and looking very weary, gaunt, and haggard. He had trudged on alone for five days, ever since, indeed, he had shaken hands near Merton with the Count de Guiscard, wished him a cheery good-bye, and promised not to mention his name (bailiffs, dear sir, the count had said) on any consideration whatever. Terribly depressed he felt. While chatting with Monsieur de Guiscard he had managed to put a screen of gaiety between himself and his reflections. But wit is a sorry comforter. To warm one's soul with a jest is analagous to warming one's hands with a cigar. All the bright bubbles with which Jonathan had covered the 'inky waves of disappointment' and worse, while good company favoured him, burst in a moment when he was left alone, and so for five days the black, naked tide had been staring up at him, uncompromisingly reminding him of what had been and of the worse there might be still in store.

Presently the park-gates caught his eye. He stopped, waited a moment, and then began to saunter backwards and forwards, up and down the road. He was screwing his courage to the sticking-point, and a terrible point it was to his proud, sensitive nature. At a distance it had not seemed so difficult to bow down before the golden calf and worship it: to humble himself in the dust and confess his

utter failure to this man who would have
no earthly sympathy with him, except as
an evidence of his own shrewd foreknow-
ledge; but here, by the park-gates, face
to face with the proofs of his utter insignificance in the eyes of a world which
always does prefer ornamental ironwork
to brains, it seemed almost impossible for
him to endorse, as it were, his own con-
demnation. Do you see how hard it was?
Jonathan Swift was a genius. The stupidity of some dozen ignorant publishers
had made him a pauper and crushed him.
Now he was coming to beg his bread from
a man who had throughout prophesied
his failure and sneered at his talents. It
was maddening. He thought of *that* and
shuddered. It might be actually maddening. What would his mother and Lauriel
do if *It* came before any provision was
made for them? No, there was no escape.
He must do it, and he must bear it too.

He calmed himself, and rang the bell.

'What do you want?' asked the porter.

'To see Sir William,' answered Jonathan, and then, recollecting his errand, he added, humbly, 'If you will allow me?'

'I don't think he will see you,' replied the man, 'but it is not my place to keep you out. You can go on to the house, and ask there.'

Then he graciously opened the portentous-looking gate, let Jonathan through, watched him for a few gawky strides down the avenue, and then went into the lodge again to pursue the more profitable occupation of making mole-traps.

Sir William was at home, and would see Jonathan Swift presently, but matters of some little importance detained him meanwhile. Such was the answer our hero got after a dreary wait with the porter. He had forgotten himself a little, and had sent up his name as Mr. Jonathan Swift.

The studied omission of the prefix he was rather thankful for than otherwise.

'It was considerate to give me the key-note to the coming interview so distinctly,' he thought, while a smile that would have gladdened Laurence Sterne to see, shone for an instant in his eye, 'very considerate.'

The key-note was going to be given more distinctly still. The illustrious negotiator of the Triple Alliance never risked being misunderstood; so a further message came down after another weary hour had dragged itself along, that probably Jonathan was hungry, in which case he could refresh himself in the buttery. The victory had been won at the park-gates. Jonathan merely bowed his assent; but there was an expression of quiet dignity in his ugly face that forced the footman to say, in defiance of orders to the contrary, as the strange figure prepared to follow him, 'This way, *sir*, if you please.'

A few of the upper servants were having their dinner in the buttery. Jonathan Swift was to rank in future as their social equal. Accepting the situation, he bowed with native politeness to his compeers, and as he did so a face caught his eye which he was fated never to forget—which was going to shape his destiny for ever. It was the face of a girl of sixteen. You must imagine her, reader. I shall not describe her. I dare not describe a woman in prose; for I am a poet, by the grace of God. And in poetry I cannot describe her, for the only poetry is the ideal, and there could be no ideal beyond her copy!

The butler, observing his glance, introduced him, 'Miss Hestor Johnson,' and the footman continued, 'Mr. Swift.' Dinner was almost over when Jonathan entered, and before many minutes the butler, civilly begging pardon for himself and the rest, left the table, leaving only Hestor, whom he asked to take care that Mr. Swift got plenty to eat and was not hurried. Jonathan had scarcely eaten since he left home, and was ravenously hungry—so hungry that he felt he must eat, though every mouthful were an insult; yet the lumps of solid, unmitigated charity seemed to choke him. He put down his knife and fork and drew his hand wearily across his brow.

'Excuse me,' he said, rising to go, 'I am very stupid to-day, I know. I have been walking, you see, for five days, and am so tired. Another time I will do my best to be more amusing.'

'Pardon me, Mr. Swift,' answered Hestor, 'I must really insist on your eating something. You are utterly worn out, and, unless you make an effort, you will probably be seriously ill to-morrow.'

As it was, Jonathan felt too ill to object

to anything; surrendering to the girlish decisiveness, he sat down again and tried to smile.

'You need this first,' went on the young hostess, pouring out a small glass of brandy and water. 'Come, you cannot say no to a lady.'

Jonathan vaguely waited a moment for a sparkling reply to occur to him, as was its wont, and then answered, simply,

'You are very good, thank you; yes, I think I do need it.'

Then there was a long pause, while Jonathan struggled laboriously to swallow some dinner, and Hestor felt rather un-comfortable at the memory of her boldness.

'Is your stay at Moor Park to be long, Mr. Swift?' she asked at length.

'I have no idea,' replied Jonathan, 'not the least. I am a very distant and very poor connection of Sir William Temple's—so distant, in fact, as to be no connection at all worth mentioning, and yet so unutterably poor, I am obliged to plead the relationship or starve. My mother, too, and my sister, they are dependent on me. I do not think for myself alone I would ask anything from anybody. Once I should have been sure; not now—not after this.'

He was scarcely speaking to her as he said this. The words conveyed a discovery to himself which absorbed his attention. No, he was not sure what limit, if any, he was determined to set to his degradation. Hester looked at him very pitifully; she, too, knew something of trials like this, young though she was; and if there is a fact in Nature, it is this, that the only portal to sympathy is sorrow—that the only feeling of compassion possible to human beings is a fellow-feeling.

Presently she said,

' Pray excuse me if I misunderstand

you, but if the post of secretary to Sir William would not be distasteful to you, I fancy he would be exceedingly glad of your assistance. He is busily employed in proving the antiquity of some Greek author or other, and '—she smiled—' you know Greek, do you not?'

Jonathan looked curiously at the young girl facing him. There was a scarcely disguised tone of confidence in her voice, which conveyed to his mind the impression that the appointment she spoke of was as much in her gift as in Sir William's, or that she thought so. Noticing his look, she added, hurriedly,

'Of course, I know nothing whatever about it, beyond the fact that Sir William has had great difficulty in obtaining the assistance he required, and that the late secretary, after the lapse of six months, is not yet succeeded.'

'That is very good news,' said Jonathan, 'but such a dignity is almost beyond my ambition and quite beyond my hopes. There is as much chance of Sir William's proving the antiquity of that Greek author himself as of his allowing me to do it for him.'

'You are bitter,' said Hestor.

'I am human,' he replied, 'and I know Greek.'

'So is, and does, Sir William,' retorted Hestor, stoutly.

'Ah! yes, equally,' was the reply. 'But pardon me,' went on Jonathan, 'I don't mean to say anything against one who has probably done a great deal for you, and towards whom, of course, your feelings must be very different from my own.'

A swift shade of colour rose in Hestor's face and died as quickly away. Jonathan saw it, and wondered what it meant.

'Yes,' she said, 'he has done a great deal for me, a very great deal. I live here amid every comfort, am well dressed, have books to read, pocket-money to spend or give away, and so on, in return for which I do absolutely nothing. You see, Mr. Johnson was Sir William's steward for very many years.'

'I quite understand,' replied Jonathan ; 'a sacred debt of gratitude paid to the father's daughter.' Nevertheless, he did *not* quite understand.

'Yes,' she answered, musingly, 'a sacred debt paid to the father's daughter.'

Jonathan felt rather afraid of the subject of conversation, so to change it he fixed on the structure instead of the substance of the last sentence.

'What a terrible language English is,' he said, 'so far as personal pronouns are concerned. One never knows except by the context who is meant by "he," "his," "him," when more than one individual is mentioned at a sitting. Possibly that accounts for the national egotism, " I," is the only pronoun which represents a person whose identity is beyond all question, and a person whose identity is beyond all question is famous, and people who are famous have a right to be egotistical Q.E.D.'

'That is a grammatical reason, Mr. Swift, but not a good one,' laughed Hestor.

'And isn't it sad to consider,' answered he, 'that it is the best one extant ?'

'Say that to Sir William,' she said, 'and he will adore you. For a man who has done so much for England, he admires his countrymen wonderfully little.'

'Marvellous !' answered Jonathan, 'almost as marvellous as that the armourer who sold a sword to a soldier at a handsome profit, yet did not love him, although the sword subsequently saved the soldier's life. And far more wonderful than that the man who conferred the public benefit of ditching (at a price) the main road from London to Westminster, yet hated both towns very cordially.'

'The price and profit account for those instances,' replied Hestor; 'but Sir William has done all he has for England, and for nothing.'

'Two things which equally deserve to be worked for,' interposed Jonathan; 'but his reward has been better than that, Miss Johnson, he has gained admiration.'

'The admiration of a mob you despise.'

'For the present,' he answered, 'but, when they admire *me*, I shall modify my opinion.'

As he spoke, the footman entered with a message that Sir William was ready to see Mr. Swift if he would step upstairs. Jonathan rose to go.

'Thank you,' he said to Hestor, 'very much indeed for having lightened my darkness as you have done this afternoon.

Pray crown your kindness by wishing that, when next I dawn upon you, it may be as the full-blown secretary of an ex-Minister of State.'

'Very willingly,' she said.

And then Jonathan went up into the awful presence, and Hestor stood by the window looking out at the fish-pond, wondering why she had taken such a fancy to the uncouth owner of the sad, ugly face; and recalling all the benefits which had been heaped upon her by Sir William Temple.

CHAPTER VI.

Sir William Temple, with all his faults, was a gentleman. He was overbearing, unsympathetic, matter-of-fact, selfish; but still a gentleman. So when the footman announced 'Mr. Swift,' and Jonathan advancing had said, 'You were right, Sir William, I was wrong,' he replied, 'I was afraid I should be. And I hope you will excuse the strong expression of my opinion on that very ground, and, if I hurt your feelings, will forget it.'

He would have said the same to his washerwoman under the same circumstances. It was his own self-respect, as a gentleman, he was considering, and of course that was a constant quantity, uninfluenced by whether the politeness was aimed at a sovereign or a slave. There was no request to be seated all this while, so Jonathan ran no risk of misunderstanding the meaning of Sir William's civility.

A moment's pause, and then,

'Well, Swift, to put disagreeable facts as agreeably as possible, I suppose you have come to me for assistance, everything else having failed you?'

'I have.'

'And yet,' went on Sir William, 'everything else has not failed you; you are a big, strong, sturdy fellow, though certainly not very soldierly in appearance—why do you not enlist?'

'I don't think,' answered Jonathan, 'that for my own part I should prefer that to starving; and so far as my poor mother and Lauriel are concerned the pay of a common soldier would not allow me even to assist their poverty.'

'Lauriel? Who is Lauriel?' was the reply. 'You have surely not been so insane as to marry on the chance of selling a few pages of satire?'

'My only sister,' answered Jonathan.

'Ah! an invalid?' queried Sir William.

'No, thank God, she is perfectly well and strong. My mother, too, enjoys fairly good health.'

'I asked,' pursued Sir William, 'because ill-health naturally occurred to me as the only pertinent objection why your mother and sister should not earn their own living.'

'That would be the only pertinent objection,' was the sad reply, 'if my strength did not constitute another and a better one than their weakness. If, besides failing, as I have already failed, I am doomed to fail more bitterly still in the effort to earn, no matter how humbly, the very few shillings necessary to help these two dear ones from the buffets of the world, then, Sir William, my mother can go charing and my sister can take a situation as a housemaid, but not till then.'

'Of course it is no business of mine,' answered he, 'but as a practical matter pardon my observing that you are being very unwise in this. You might fail, as you have suggested; you might die. What is then to become of your helpless relatives unused to help themselves? Take common-sense advice when you can get it. Tell your mother that the battle of life is hard enough to fight when one's arms are free, much more when one is bound as you propose to be: say that she must provide for herself as best she can, and that your sister must do so too; then you will be in a position to accept such a situation as you have some chance of being offered.'

'Spare me, please spare me,' answered Jonathan. 'You do not mean that, you cannot mean it; it is only said to humble me; but, God knows, I am humbled in the dust already.'

'Excuse me contradicting you,' was the curt reply, 'I never say what I do not mean, except diplomatically, and that, you will admit, is altogether beyond the present question. However, I am to understand that my advice is distasteful. Very well, you will agree with me some day; and now, what next? Do you want money?'

Jonathan drew himself up a little.

'No,' he said, 'I am not a beggar—yet —not in its baldest sense, at least. No, I do not wish money, except in return for some service which I trust I can render. It is employment I seek, Sir William. I do trust you can give me some, almost anything, no matter what.'

'You are a poet, are you not? But, let me see—the book you showed me was not poetry, was it? It was prose, if I remember rightly.'

'It was prose,' answered Jonathan, 'still, I must confess, I think myself a poet. Very likely I am wrong.'

'That is rather beside the point, however,' was the reply. 'I rather meant by my question that your tastes were literary, purely literary. You could not, for example, undertake to superintend the execution of some extensive land drainage I am about to carry out?'

'If no other employment with which I am conversant occurs to you, I will superintend the drainage only too gladly,' answered the poet; 'and as to my capabilities——'

'In short, you cannot do it, if you would,' put in Sir William:

'Perhaps a few days' experience——'
was the pleading answer.

Alas, poor Jonathan, how he yearned
for this occupation, which promised him
the work and pay of a superior navvy.

'True; but in the meantime the lawns
and terraces might be ruined for years.
Well, I scarcely know, besides that, what
I can offer you. I am far from being a
rich man. My position will not warrant
me in building a niche simply that you
may occupy it, were I ever so desirous
of doing so. At the same time, if you
care to change your mind as to a gift—
and, for my own part, I really fail to see
any tangible difference between accepting
money for nothing, and accepting it in
payment for services which are artificial
and useless—you can ask the steward for
ten pounds. I trust you will quite understand, nevertheless, that that is the limit
of my bounty. By taking the money, it

is clearly to be borne in mind, you give me an implicit discharge of any claims, real or imaginary, you believe you have upon me.'

'No, thank you, Sir William,' said Jonathan, speaking very slowly and quietly. 'I would take it, if I could, for my mother's sake, but I cannot. Then there is nothing? All my torture has been for nothing. I have grovelled in the dust for nothing. Yet you can be kind, humane, generous. You have treated the daughter of your dead servant, kindly, humanely, generously——'

'What, in the name of all that is occult, does that matter to you?' irritably interposed Sir William.

'Well, good-bye, I will go. I must not waste any time. Five days have passed uselessly already. I will ask strangers for work ; or, if I must beg, I will beg from strangers.'

And the tall, gaunt figure turned to the door, and strode gloomily away without another word. Back to the entrance-hall went Jonathan, and there paused hesitating. He had left his hat in the buttery when summoned to meet Sir William, and he did not at all relish the idea of going there to fetch it. Something warned him that his girl hostess was there, still standing by the oriel window and wondering whether the bitter scholar had been offered his much-wished-for secretaryship, and he was loth to tell her that he had been found incompetent to take charge of draining the kitchen-garden, and had been offered ten pounds to go away and promise never to come back. He waited some time to see if anyone willing to get his hat for him would chance to come. Fate had decreed otherwise. He did not wait long, the house seemed to stifle him. He longed to leave it and its memories behind him; so, acting on a sudden impulse, he opened the door and stood, as he had expected, in the presence of Hestor Johnson.

'I think I left my hat here,' he said; 'and, before I go, allow me to thank you again for your kindness.'

'Might I ask you to do me a favour, Mr. Swift?' was the reply.

'Anything in my power,' he answered, with a grim smile to himself, as he recollected how little that was.

'It is certainly in your power,' answered Hestor; 'it is to wait here a few minutes while I bring you something I am particularly anxious you should see.'

Jonathan bowed.

'Thank you,' said Hestor, as she left the room to go straight upstairs to the door out of which our hero so lately came, with a fresh sword in his spirit, a fresh drop of bitterness polluting his soul.

Arrived there, she looked round her as though to make sure she was alone, and then entered. Five minutes later she returned again to the buttery with a light heart and sparkling eyes.

'I cannot find what I wanted,' she said, 'but I met Sir William, who says he wishes to see you again for a moment before you go.   Will you please go now?'

Jonathan stared in amazement.

'Please go now,' she reiterated. 'Sir William is going out, and may miss you. But as a favour to me,' she interposed, 'and to acquit you of any obligation to me for making you eat your dinner.'

'I obey,' said Jonathan ; 'but first good-bye, and again thank you.'

Tritest of reflections ! '*how a straw may influence our destiny,*' what a load of arrant absurdity generations of mock philosophers have piled upon thy back ! Oh ! the children who have crushed towns beneath avalauches; the little ditches which have decided the fates of empires; the molehills which have altered the destiny of the world! Rubbish, you wretched symposium, at which there is neither philosophy nor dinner. It was a child, and the force of gravitation, which hurled the seething mass of boiling rock down to its destiny. It was bad generalship, inferior forces, *and* the ditch which lost the battle; and, if King William had died of a fever or the small-pox, who on earth would have suggested that his disease bore any conceivable relation to this precious 'straw'? And why is the death of a great man more a straw when he dies of a molehill than when he dies of the measles? A result is never more than commensurate with its cause. You can get energy out of nothing, no more in the moral world than in the physical, and it is madness to expect you can. When Clive's pistol missed fire, it did not save India, any more than all the bullets which missed him afterwards, and all the diseases he did not have, saved India.

Pray pardon this digression, but Jonathan Swift's position might suggest the 'strawic' craze to some one, and I am anxious to guard against any such contingency.

Sir William had put on his hat, and was going out, as Jonathan reached the study.

'I had forgotten,' he said, 'that a work on which I am engaged—Greek—requires some transcribing, verification, &c. If you are sufficiently a Greek scholar, and if you choose to accept the office, *and position*, of my private secretary, I am willing to give you a trial. At the same time, it must be distinctly understood that you will be my secretary, and not my relative or friend.'

Then, without waiting for an answer, he walked on, down the passage, down the stairs, out into the garden. Jonathan, with a tumult of contending passion in his breast, flung himself into a chair.

'Ah!' he exclaimed, bitterly apostrophising the absent baronet, 'if it were as easy to be your secretary as not to be your friend, the office would be a sinecure.'

CHAPTER VII.

FATE was weaving a gigantic web round Jonathan Swift. He was a big fly, and required a big web. A very little scorn, misjudgment, obloquy are enough to crush a poor weakling, whether in the world of letters or elsewhere. Even as little as the flail of some hack critic, the unknown and unknowable discerner of good and evil on the staff of a weekly paper, is too much for some. Ignoring the fact that the only brilliant thing about—say, for instance, the dramatic critic of the *Bathenæum*, is the rapidity with which his remarks are forgotten, some people, silly in this respect if in no other, have allowed these remarks to kill them. God grant that, when I am fatally run over, it may be by a railway train, not by a donkey-cart!

Jonathan Swift was, I repeat, a very big fly. To fairly crush him required all the efforts of Dulness and her satellites; so she wove a very big web, and Monsieur the Count de Guiscard was one of the strongest meshes in the web she wove. It may be necessary to mention this for fear anyone should suspect me of digressing from the thread of my biography in saying so much about this soldier of fortune and his doings. Wait, reader; for he who can wait circles the world without an effort.

Monsieur de Guiscard, after wishing Jonathan good-bye on the morning when they parted, walked briskly down the high road towards Merton, until a turn fairly hid his route from view, and then at ouce made his way through the hedge into an oak plantation, and sauntered leisurely back in the direction of Mrs. Swift's cottage. He did not dare to remain on the public road one minute longer than was absolutely necessary, and yet he was sadly afraid that Jonathan also might by some accident retrace his steps. To avoid the barest possibility of a meeting, he picked out a fallen tree in a well-sheltered nook, seated himself upon it, and waited. From where he sat he could see obliquely down a steep gully and over the tops of the farther saplings far away to the horizon, where the rearguard of the storm mustered its thick clouds angrily against the deep blue sky. I will tell you what he was thinking of as he gazed with eyes, which did not seem to see, at the misty battlements and turrets ; for it will help you to understand him.

He was thinking of a moss-grown castle in Picardy, standing with giant walls and blade-like windows, the end of a long vista through a vale of chestnut-trees; and there upon the lawn, by the light—not dim enough, alas!—of the hazy moon, he saw a youth and a maiden. He is pleading in vain an honourable love, yet he is noble, and she is only beautiful—no, not only so, for she loved him too. And the youth, how he adored that village angel, and how he adored her memory still! Monsieur de Guiscard knew, for he remembered—for it was he.

'No, no,' she is saying, 'you are mad— it would ruin you. I will save you—I will go. Henri, Henri, kiss me before I go away for ever!'

The first and last. The great door swings open suddenly: there is a rush of liveried assassins, and behind them, through the sombre archway, is seen the old marquis, pallid with rage at the degradation of his only son : then a scuffle, a frantic curse, as the young lord is seized, disarmed, and sees in his helplessness that some one of his father's servants has bettered the instructions of their master ' to alarm, only to alarm,' and that his second life is lying dead, dead, dead before him. And then the cloisters where the broken-hearted abbot of twenty-five had striven to dig with missal and rosary a tomb deep enough for his grief, and, failing, had plunged into mad vice black enough to disgrace even the place and the times. Then the degradation, gentle in consideration of the blue blood coursing in the young man's veins ; degradation gilded with a cavalry command, but degradation still, and acting as such, debasing as such. And then from bad to worse through all the devious paths of private wickedness, public infamy, to a soldier's treachery, detection, flight.

Monsieur de Guiscard, pale and agitated, rose from his seat.

'I can never own even her grave again,' he said aloud to himself; 'I can never be buried beside her if I fail in this. Nothing else will gain me pardon, and I need favour. Succeed I must.'

As he spoke, he drew from his pocket a small bottle curiously arranged in two divisions, one containing a thin roll of paper and the other a powerful acid, the object, of course, being that, if the stopper were removed by one unacquainted with the secret the writing on the paper should be at once destroyed. Carefully extracting the scroll and unfolding it, Monsieur de Guiscard feasted his eyes on the instructions which gave him one more chance of living and dying other than an outcast and a felon in the eyes of the world.

They ran thus, and were in the handwriting of the French king, though signed by the Stuart exile :

'You will use every means of rescuing our subjects from the tyranny of the usurper who is alone and personally responsible for his misdeeds and the punishment for which he deserves to personally bear.

'JAMES.'

'A desperate work,' he thought, with a sigh, as he replaced the precious document in its resting-place, 'and in desperate hands. I wish k-i-l-l had not been spelt in so many letters, it would have been more significant of confidence—however—' And, dismissing the vain regret, he resumed his walk towards his base of operations.

The royal progression through England had been arranged for some time in the summer of 1695, and the pretended route to be followed had been ostentatiously made public, as though to show how completely the king trusted even his enemies. The expedition was in reality neither more or less than a gigantic personal canvass, designed to influence, so far as such means could do so, the impending parliamentary elections, and on that ground, if on no other, all *appearance* of caution had to be carefully excluded.

William the Deliverer knew exceedingly well that his life was always menaced : that a faction as insignificant as it was desperate would never desist, while his life prolonged their opportunity, from thirsting after his blood. He estimated their menaces, their hatred, their perseverance, precisely at what these were worth. When no reason to the contrary existed, every precaution against danger was freely taken ; but the moment that circumstances showed these precautions themselves to involve greater danger—that of calling the attention of the nation to the isolation of a bayonet-protected king—then, at once he called his guards, as it were, from protecting himself to protect his people.

It was pretty generally understood, consequently, that the royal progression about to take place would be a very modest affair in so far as the central authorities were concerned. The guards of honour, the yeomen, the constables, would be just such as the respective counties chose to furnish, and, if any district chanced to be sufficiently disloyal, the king and his attendants would drive through that district with very little more pomp and circumstance than would ordinary gentlemen.

Monsieur de Guiscard knew all this of course before we became acquainted with him at the door of Mrs. Swift's cottage—

it was why he was there. Logic is rarely an important factor in desperate enterprises, of whatever sort. There is a point in odds beyond which calculation seems only a laborious method of finding out the certainty of uncertainty, and, as a natural consequence, the more hopelessly difficult the enterprise, the less clearly defined very often is the scheme on which he who has undertaken it relies for his success.

This was pre-eminently the case with Monsieur de Guiscard. From the moment he had received the death-warrant we have watched him reading, and had been informed of the glorious reward its execution would entail upon himself, he had been possessed by the determination to accomplish his purpose on the theatre on which we see him. *How*, so far he had scarcely considered, and why he should have chosen Merton in preference to any other equally secluded spot was a psychological problem he had taken no trouble to fathom. The only clear idea, indeed, that Monsieur de Guiscard had was that from the moment he put his foot on English soil, he must keep very well hidden. He had done so. When the storm caught him in Merton woods, he had been more than a week in England, and yet had excited suspicion in nobody. He was beginning to distrust his good luck. It could not last for ever, and on the scene of his intended exploit the difficulties to be encountered, and especially the grand difficulty of keeping entirely out of sight, loomed up big and threatening. Such was his case when he was driven by the hurricane to take shelter in Mrs. Swift's cottage.

We have seen how he availed himself of the unexpected opportunity. The conversation of the Swifts soon disclosed to him that they were precisely the individuals on whom most reliance could be placed to keep the secret of his presence, if they had a good enough reason for doing so; and when he found that Jonathan was going away almost immediately, and probably for long, the course to follow seemed so distinct that Monsieur de Guiscard took it without a thought. The story Lauriel heard from the persecuted soldier of fortune, was, of course, a gigantic fabrication, designed purely and simply to excite her compassion, and afford a reason for Monsieur de Guiscard's otherwise incomprehensible desire for rigid seclusion from the outside world. As such it had answered its purpose admirably, and, as he strolled back to the cottage, the only doubt in the mind of the would-be regicide was whether all the purpose in the world would enable him to support the insufferable *ennui* of such an imprisonment as now lay before him.

'Ah,' sighed he, 'it is a terrible thing not to be able to be even consistently miserable for ten consecutive minutes— and it is very French.'

As he approached the cottage, he saw Lauriel in the little garden which adjoined it, busily employed in repairing, so far as she could, the damage wrought by the storm. The thick privet-hedge which shut in the tiny plot had been in several places crushed and broken by limbs blown from the trees which had fallen on it. Lauriel stopped in despair before one great gap through which projected a bough that had not long ago been the chiefest glory of a grand old oak.

'I can never move that,' she said to herself, 'and if I could, the gap would be there still. How unfortunate!' she mused, looking at the footway outside the hedge; 'passers-by can see in at our windows now

—that is, when there are any passers-by;
and if but one of the villagers saw Monsieur de Guiscard! How long he is re-
turning—can he have been discovered ?'

The poor girl shuddered at the thought,
and glanced down the wood in the direction of Merton. The first object her gaze
encountered was, of course, the subject of
her meditation, Monsieur de Guiscard himself, standing just outside the wicket-gate,
and regarding her with eyes in which pen-
sive admiration was mingled with sadness
in most captivating proportions. The
admiration offered by distress is naturally
felt to be the highest form of commenda-
tion, but Lauriel was too anxious about
Monsieur de Guiscard's safety to even
notice his expression.

' Pray come in,' she cried; ' you must
not run unnecessary risk. Have you been
seen this morning ?'

' I think not,' he answered. ' Oh ! Miss

Swift, how it galls me to have to take the precautions of a felon! It is scarcely better than to be one. But come, my better nature has not all been crushed out of me by a heartless persecution yet—not yet; I will not give you the pain of keeping even so trifling a secret as my story is from your mother a moment longer. Ugh! it is horrible to have to hide anything, but —oneself——! Do you know, I told the first lie that ever passed my lips to your brother this morning? I asked him not to mention my name anywhere, I prayed him not to, indeed, and, unaccustomed to concealment, did it so clumsily that he asked me why. "Bailiffs," I said— "bailiffs!"'

Monsieur de Guiscard's handsome face clouded drearily at the memory of such a blot upon his honour.

'I wish,' said Lauriel, 'it had not been unsafe to tell Jonathan,' and then, as the thought suddenly struck her, she turned round and added, 'What possessed you to tell us your real name?'

There was a reproachful ring in Monsieur de Guiscard's voice as, looking her straight in the face and drawing his hand wearily across his brow, he answered,

'I deserve the implied rebuke, Miss Swift, and I feel it bitterly. Yes, if I told your brother a lie, I might have told you one too.'

The scientists—the men whose souls are not manufactured in Birmingham—generally talk, when they have exhausted their stock of electricity and evolution, about latent heat. There is a great deal of latent evidence in certainty, which explains the connection of my ideas. Monsieur de Guiscard had told his story throughout with such tact and skill that it had never occurred to Lauriel to question his veracity, yet it would have required nothing but a breath to inspire her with doubt. This last touch, however, was certainty, which corresponded to latent heat in steam. The north wind of suspicious circumstance would have to blow for long before it cooled the warm trust inspired by Monsieur de Guiscard's masterpiece, 'I might have told you one too!'

If one wishes to talk sense, one is generally obliged to be original. That is a mercy. As an exception, allow me to remark that nothing is more unfailingly infectious than confidence, than trust (except, by the way, its antithesis), and that Monsieur de Guiscard was very well aware of the fact. So, as they passed the narrow doorway, he felt that victory was won, and was not in the least astonished at his success when an hour later Mrs. Swift, as tenderly concerned about his fate as was her daughter, escorted him to the room Jonathan had lately occupied, and which was to be his domicile until the storm should cease to grumble, and the clouds should roll away.

CHAPTER VIII.

A WEEK or so after Jonathan Swift had left home, Lauriel found awaiting her in Merton, upon the occasion of one of her forced marches, as she was wont to term her little relished journeys to the village, a letter, and a small parcel from her brother. Hastily dispatching her commissions, she ran home with the new-found treasures, determined not to open them until her mother could jointly have the delight of investigating whatever of good news they might contain. She had scarcely started, however, before she stopped again and hesitated. The letter had come to Merton by a carrier who was also a dealer in various kinds of fancy goods, and, among other things, in tobacco. Now Lauriel's womanly eyes had noticed that Monsieur de Guiscard had lately been smoking but half a pipe in the course of twenty-four hours, and she surmised that probably it was because his stock of the divine narcotic was nearly all offered. She beat her pretty little foot upon the ground and doubted. There was no money in her purse—not any. Her mother would so much enjoy opening that parcel from Jonathan. But Monsieur de Guiscard——. So she opened it, and there being money in it, as she had expected, bought a small parcel of tobacco, and then trotted off through the wood as fast as possible.

' You see,' she was saying to herself, as, with sparkling eyes and cheeks flushed by her haste, she entered the cottage, ' the letter is the great thing, mamma can open that: and Monsieur de Guiscard must be so terribly dull only getting out when it is dark. He is so kind and thoughtful, too, for others, that one surely ought to think of him a little in return. Yes, mamma can open *my* letter instead.' There was presently an amicable discussion on this point between Mrs. Swift and her daughter. 'But,' urged Lauriel, 'I will open the parcel for my share,' and, the little ruse succeeding, Lauriel, under cover of a gleeful laugh, mentioned to her mother about the tobacco purchase, and begged her to give it to Monsieur de Guiscard.

'Why not give it to him yourself, my dear?' answered Mrs. Swift. 'The thought was yours, you should have the credit of it.'

Lauriel could not say why not, so she struck a theatrical attitude, laughed more gleefully than ever, and cried,

' Behold, oh! world, the great impersona-
tion of every virtue—no, no, mamma, the
credit of half a pound of tobacco would be
my apotheosis. Jonathan says, mamma,
you always want to find out the first cause
of everything, and he says the first cause
of everything is—I don't know. I wonder
what he says in his letter.' So they fell
to work to read it, and it ran as follows :

' MY DEAR LITTLE SISTER,

   ' A secretary writes that some
one else may not write, not that anybody
may read ; and I am turning thoroughly
official. So rejoice in this, probably the
last letter you will receive from me, not
because this is the last but because the last
one wasn't.

' As a proof of my growing appreciation
of Sir William's trinity—order, method, and
himself—I send you along with this three
weeks' wages, to the amount of £4 2s. 4d.,

neatly stowed away in a cardboard box, labelled in red ink, and given me by the great ex-minister's butler. Remember, Lauriel, I trust you. You promised me ! No more washing Steinkirks ; no more spoiling those pretty little white fingers for the sake of a great ugly brother who is rapidly finding out that his only merit consists in having such a mother and sister. £4 2s. 4d. is not a gigantic sum by any manner of means, but living as you do—very wretchedly, that is to say—it will supply you until I can send more. God knows how thankful I am to be able to do even this little towards my duty and my love. For, do you know, I am very fond of you indeed, my little sister. But, on consideration, the chances are that you do not know ; for I was not at all clear on the point myself until last night, when, in a dream—now don't laugh, Lauriel, my blood curdles—I saw an infinite maze, woven, as it were, of curved rays of light, and stretching like a web throughout all space; and as I lay wondering what this could be, and looking earnestly at it, I saw that another web crossed through the first as the woof crosses the warp, but its threads were black, like the tissue of outer darkness.

'Wondering still more, I gazed still more earnestly, and at length I observed that the lines near to where I stood were vibrating rapidly, although the motion was no longer discernible at a very little distance onwards. Turning round to understand the cause of this agitation, I became aware that along each ray there was travelling a "something" which I could see but could not comprehend—at least, not so long as it continued to move; but each grew still, sooner or later, and then, although the substance was never apparent, one could tell the shape and read the letters which the mazy path it had journeyed along had worn upon it. And on some I could see, " Eternal influence for good," and of these the rays stretching before them could be followed as far as the eye could reach ; but on others it was, " Throughout all time for evil," and the rays before these reached a very little way—only, indeed, to where a great river of infinite whiteness, springing in full flood at once from a jasper rock, caught them in its waves, and so deflected them that they too became as the others.

' Now, as I watched these indescribable somewhats, ever more and more amazed, I noticed that there was none but what travelled in harmony with some others, suiting its mazy path to their sinuosities ; indeed, it seemed that cadence was a condition of their existence. And not only was this individual, but while each moved regularly with its group, each group moved also in cadence with another, and so on as far as my grasp permitted me to follow. Observing this, I remembered what Plato had said, and, ceasing to allow myself to be absorbed in watching alone, I began to listen intently. Strangely enough, I could hear nothing. That there was music, I could *see*, but I could not hear one note.

'Then in my dream I was sad and wept, and through my tears I became aware of something in front of me, behind me, around me, which I could not see, while my eyes were dry. It was a Spirit infinite, eternal, unchangeable, in His being, wisdom, power, holiness, justice, goodness, and truth; and through my tears, which reduced and diminished like a lens what was far too great for me to see without them, I saw that He was tuning all the motions of each individual and group to

the sound of Himself as it rung in a reed
called Love.

'Strangely enough I trembled to see it,
for I slept; and, Lauriel, we all sleep here.
I saw that a higher than fate, a more
necessary than necessity, demanded the
existence of those black, black lines.
There needed " discords to complete the
music." Just then I heard it; for I had
caught a breath from the reed and was
inspired by Love. The web close to me
was vibrating strongly; a music was ring-
ing out far too clearly, far too sweetly. I
knew it, I knew it was yours, and I could
not help; and the discord, the pitchy
darkness came, as the love that looked
in sleep so fearfully like cruelty directed
and mingled with the clear, bright note,
with you, and hushed it till the other
side of the great white river should be
reached. Then I awoke, chilled to the
soul, and, Lauriel, can you wonder that

I know now how very much I love you?'

'Silly fellow,' laughed Lauriel, as much to reassure herself as to soothe her mother. 'If he must turn prophet as well as poet, we shall have to change his name from Jonathan to David. What a bad letter he writes, mamma, not a word about anything one wishes to know. I had far rather be told what he actually had for dinner than what he imagines I am going to have for destiny! However, we may infer it was pork. Now, to proceed. I really believe that there is some news, after all—listen.

' "To change, begging your pardon, a disagreeable subject, while avoiding going from bad to worse by omitting all reference to Sir William Temple and his Greek inquiries, I am driven to inform you that there is a young lady here of very pre-

possessing appearance and agreeable manners. It is quite within the bounds of
possibility that she is neither the one nor
the other when anywhere else, but *here*
she is undoubtedly both. One thinks so
much more of a lamp on a dark night
than in the day time. There is a great
deal, too, in the circumstances under
which an acquaintanceship is made, and
it is odd how coincident have been my
meetings with this damsel, and my strokes
of good fortune. It was immediately after
seeing her that Sir William elected me to
the influential and lucrative post I occupy;
and so with twenty other occurrences.
Something is going wrong—I see, by accident, Miss Johnson, mention what it is,
and it goes right straightway. In fact,
to be honest, I am growing superstitious,
and tell her all manner of grievances,
hopes, etcetera, with a lurking belief
that the mere fact of doing so will be

an irresistible reason for a happy issue.
And remember that it must be necromancy
or nothing—neck or nothing—for, though
I call her a lady, and though she is one
in every other respect, she is not so by
birth by any manner of means, being only
the daughter of the great man's late
butler.

' " Sir William—who has his good points
after all—is very kind to her, out of consideration to her father's memory, and as
a somewhat tardy return for his long and
faithful services. She does what she likes,
goes where she likes; gets a little pocket-money occasionally, which she either
spends on books or gives away, and *voilà
tout*, as those people say who, having a
scanty knowledge of their own language,
are fain to eke it out with another. You
see, of course, that poor Miss Johnson is
really worse off than I am, and has as
little real influence. However, I have

become possessed with the idea, thanks to a sequence of accidents, that she is potential energy itself, and like her in proportion to her apparent great beneficence."

'Oh!' said Lauriel. 'Oh!' chimed her mother. That was all.

'Now,' went on the letter, 'good-bye. There is a great deal left to say, but I must insist on adhering to my theory. The tail of a letter ought to be, like the tail of everything else in Nature, the thinnest part of the body; but then, further, I detest anything thin, especially in literature, so I save my consistence by emulating the two grandest objects in the world—a man and a guinea-pig—and leave the tail out altogether.'

'Not a word about the poor boy's dinner, nor whether they have given him a comfortable room,' said Mrs. Swift.

'I shall open a correspondence with Miss Johnson and find out,' was the reply. And so the sitting terminated.

CHAPTER IX.

MONSIEUR DE GUISCARD had not been idle during his fortnight's residence with the Swifts; he had thought a great deal. With most men it is much better to act without thinking than to think without acting, because the chances are that, though they *may do* something by accident worth doing, they will never through all eternity think anything worth thinking. I wish the whole genus of those creatures which the education of the nineteenth century has carved out of so-and-so many hundredweights of flesh and blood, and who *call themselves* 'earnest thinkers,' would take this fact to heart. I mean for their own sakes; they do exceedingly little harm to other people.

Monsieur de Guiscard, however, was a good deal above the average, and thought to some purpose; besides, he had got something to think about, which, after all, is one of the great difficulties in the way of so many. From having a confused, indistinct idea that his own character was to be restored, or at least whitewashed, somehow, thanks to King William being got rid of, somehow, he had arrived at a pretty clear notion of how this consummation was to be brought about.

One of the very few men in England on whom Monsieur de Guiscard could count for hearty support in any scheme he chose to concoct, having for its object the overturn of William the Deliverer and the Protestant succession, was James, Lord

Vane of Vane Castle. Now Vane Castle was the home of Lauriel's Steinkirks, and was within two miles of Mrs. Swift's cottage. When Monsieur de Guiscard sailed from France on the errand we are considering, he was well aware that he had not been asked to undertake so illustrious, if dangerous, a task until the honour and risk had been declined by almost every Jacobite of greater respectability than himself; and he also knew that one of the very few exceptions, one of the men who had not been asked, and who would have attempted the feat if he had been, was Lord Vane; and the reason was that King James did not understand Lord Vane, who prided himself upon being what we should now call 'a philosophical radical,' and, as a necessary consequence, did not trust him. But the reader will have no difficulty in understanding the poor ex-monarch's objection when he knows the master of Vane Castle better. Meanwhile, it is sufficient to observe that his knowledge of the opinions and character of Lord Vane had partly directed the count by a kind of instinctive preference towards the district in which he lived.

'I observed some turrets during my walk this evening,' Monsieur de Guiscard remarked, a few days after his arrival, to Lauriel. 'Who lives in that eyrie, and how does he like it?' And in a very few minutes he had assured himself that it was, as the absence of any other suitable residence had led him to imagine, the place he was in search of.

Up to the time at which this chapter begins, however, the count had not introduced himself to his desired co-conspirator. If chickens do not hatch in three weeks, they certainly will not in a month, he had wisely considered, and had therefore not risked sharing his scheme with anyone a moment sooner than necessity demanded. Now, however, he had done all he could do alone, and without better information than the news, letters Lauriel borrowed from the village afforded; so, choosing a dark night, he launched the rickety lifeboat of his fortunes on the troubled waters of conspiracy.

That night Lord Vane was in his library, stretched in an easy-chair, reading the 'Hind and Panther,' when a servant entered and handed him a sealed envelope. The baron was on his feet in an instant; he knew the seal.

'Who brought this?' he asked.

'I don't know, my lord,' replied the man; 'he said there was no answer, but if you wished to send any message he would step upstairs.'

'Certainly,' was the answer.

So, a moment later, the Count de Guiscard and Lord Vane were face to face, and fate began another thread in the big web she was weaving for our hero.

'In accordance with the contents of this,' began Lord Vane, indicating the letter he had opened in the meantime, 'I offer you a hearty welcome, only qualified by the regret that none of my countrymen is prepared to serve the public good as, I imagine, are you, a foreigner (or the king would not have written this).'

'I will do anything,' replied De Guiscard, 'that I can, and that is right, to fulfil the wishes of my king and yours.' And then, looking round, 'Might I ask, my lord, whether conversation here is absolutely safe?'

'Quite,' affably returned the other, 'except as being between a full man and a fasting one. You must be hungry—you have come far, no doubt. By the way, where have you come from, and how?'

'Place, manner, time,' cheerily answered

De Guiscard, who was not at all anxious to give any information on this score until he was quite sure of his ground. 'The coast, skulked by night, and, to be frank, I *am* hungry, and more especially that variety of hunger which is known as thirst. I suppose, my lord, that because our business is serious is no reason for our being so too?'

Lord Vane laughed.

'Do you see what I am doing?' he said, pulling a handle. 'This is a bell hung on a wire communicating with the servants' hall. An improvement that, is it not, on the barbarous custom, not only of our ancestors, but even of so many around us, who, refusing to believe that change and evil are not synonymous, deny themselves the benefits of modern progress. Yet some day,' he continued, with a sigh, which told only too plainly the pleasure he derived from having his invention to himself, 'every haberdasher in Cheapside will call his apprentice this way.'

'Ah!' metaphorically answered De Guiscard, 'improve bells as much as you like, but stick to a handle to ring them by.'

'Yes, I am quite clear about that,' said Lord Vane. 'And now, while you are dining, you won't care to talk, and, as theory should always precede practice, I will seize the favourable opportunity of explaining on what principles alone any such enterprise as that which I think you meditate can be justified.'

'Do you think,' doubtfully objected De Guiscard, 'that the road matters, if the goal be the same?'

'Beyond all doubt it does,' was the reply; 'for unless one knows the road by which another is travelling, one never can be sure of the goal.'

'True,' acquiesced De Guiscard, seeing

objection useless, but dubious as to whether abstract politics or theology would improve his claret. 'True.'

'I shall not be long,' continued the good-natured peer; 'for nothing is true which cannot be proved in ten minutes. And now for my principles. You will understand, however, that, although I am just now convinced of the justness of my conclusions, and am willing to risk life, fortune, everything in their defence, yet I am well aware of the fallibility of human reason, and shall welcome any criticism on any point in which you may detect a flaw. I hold, then, with the old philosophers that the only thing worth living for is happiness, and that, therefore, the pursuit of happiness should be the main object of life. Of course it follows that government, as a human institution, is a machine for manufacturing happiness for those governed, and I am certain, thanks to careful historical investigation, that a despotic monarchy best fulfils this condition. Now, I believe, on the other hand, in the absolute right of a majority to do as they please with both themselves and other people, and I confess that for long it puzzled me how to reconcile the two propositions. I think, however, that it can be done thus —and it is an essential element of despotic government, after all—you must force the majority to agree with you.'

'Capital,' laughed De Guiscard.

'Stay now,' interrupted Lord Vane. 'I am serious, and, as I believe, strictly logical. Consider. No one denies the right of anybody to bring anybody else to his way of thinking, on such a subject for instance as this, by pointing out to him the inevitable consequences of popular government: its revolutions, disturbances, mob-tyrannies, or, in other words, by appealing to his fears. Now, what more do I do if I take a pistol, present it at whom it may concern, and tell him to agree with me or be shot? I still only appeal to his fears. What I mean is this. The "majority" argument rests altogether on a physical basis. If I admitted any distinction between a physical appeal to the fear or other passion of a British elector and a mental one, I should, of course, to be consistent, have to stop estimating a "majority" by units of flesh and blood. I am a thorough-going democrat, however, and the only peculiarity about me is that I am a consistent one.'

'You are quite right, so far,' replied De Guiscard; and then, as a leading question, 'Suppose you had to shoot the man in question?'

'My right to do that,' answered Lord Vane, 'would entirely depend on whether or not I had a reasonable chance of subsequent success in obtaining a majority; for of course the majority confers the right, if I have it with me at the time, or, which is precisely the same thing, can retrospectively confer it, if it comes over to me afterwards. As to this right, there can be no doubt whatever, or what would be the meaning of the word "rebel," and what the justification of hanging, drawing, and quartering?'

'And,' said De Guiscard, facing round, 'what is our chance?'

'You are either a very bold or a very desperate man to talk about such subjects with a perfect stranger,' returned Lord Vane. 'Ah! I see you think we are very much on a par as to that; but remember, the present government of England restricts itself as much as possible to hanging foreigners, that they would much rather win my support than cut off my

head, and lastly, that my word would
hang you, while *vice versâ* it is not
so.'

'So be it,' returned De Guiscard, who
knew a good deal more about the man he
was addressing than Lord Vane imagined.
'I am quite happy in your hands; while
as to you in mine, read that'—handing
his scroll,—'and allow me to distinctly
inform you that I am in England to carry
out my master's command as therein implied, and your master's wish as therein
expressed.'

'How?'

'It is partly to enable me to answer
that question that I have done myself the
honour to wait upon you,' replied the
count.

'Say rather you have done *me*, Monsieur
le Comte,' graciously returned the other.
'Well, I suppose you have no objection to
tyrannicide?'

De Guiscard stared. This cool, argumentative way of putting the matter fairly took away his breath.

'I beg your pardon,' pursued Lord Vane, evidently annoyed; 'but I understood you to agree with the propositions I laid down a few minutes ago, in which case the other follows as of course.'

De Guiscard, scarcely recovered from his amazement, simply bowed.

'And observe this,' went on the irrepressible logician; 'if a man prefers his liberty to his life, he has a clear right to do so, and to die as much in defence of his liberty as in defence of his life; but notice, there is no moral difference between one life and another, so if a man may murder himself to escape from slavery— or, which is the same thing, rise in arms when he is morally certain to be beaten— he may take anybody else's life with the same end. Or again, consider this, and escape from the conclusion if you can. If a man may take another's life in defence of his own, may he not take it in defence of what makes his life his own, his liberty?'

'Undoubtedly you are right,' said De Guiscard, who had recovered the use of his tongue. 'What startled me a little was your business-like way of putting a subject which, after all, is scarcely pleasant.'

'Nay,' said Lord Vane, 'nothing is really unpleasant which can be proved to be right, and I pride myself on never shrinking from a logical conclusion, *let it be what it please.* Thank you, yes, I will take a glass of claret. Now, there being no abstract objection to tyrannicide, it remains to be considered whether there are any practical ones.'

Monsieur de Guiscard was a little puzzled what to say. He had come to propound a definite scheme and obtain the means of carrying it into effect; but he was too shrewd a man of the world not to estimate Lord Vane at his true value after such a conversation, and he hesitated before communicating his tissue of human passion to a syllogistic automaton. People are apt to deride passion as being a fluctuating, uncertain thing, and to compare it in this respect at a great disadvantage with reason. There is no accounting for such a thing but by the eternal necessity of error. Go back to history; I would ask all those of whom it is worth a wise man's while to ask anything, go back to history, go back to your own experience even, and tell me whether it is reason or passion which has had the most real influence upon mankind, upon yourself? Was it reason which decided 'Homoousion'? Tell me, oh! Constantine, great emperor, who never understood the point at issue. Or the

Reformation?   Say, Jenny Geddes of
wooden argument memory.   Or the Revolution?   Deny it, Shaftesbury, with blood
on your fingers; and you, Sydney, with
coppers in your pocket; and you, Halifax,
greatest of statesmen, grandest of men,
because—you know I am right.   And tell
me, Voltaire, had *you*, concerned in *your*
revolution, six intelligent disciples?   Monsieur de Guiscard knew very well that syl-
logisms were not to be relied on as a basis
for estimating anyone's course of conduct.
Better ones might supplant them at any
moment; but feeling is constant, always
for long, and generally for life.   So, I repeat, he was puzzled what to reply to
Lord Vane's question.   Presently he said,

'The locality is good, is it not, for such
an attempt?'

'Very,' answered Lord Vane. ' *We* shall
not do this exceedingly limited monarch
much honour, and as for the common peo-

ple, their loyalty is greater than their enterprise, and beyond a gift of Merton ale, or
some absurdity of that sort, they will do
nothing. So the guard of honour, or dis-
honour, as you please, will probably not be
enormous. We two, thanks to the near
approach to which I should be entitled,
could make a certainty of the affair with
short concealed blunderbusses. Of course
the chances are we should be taken, but
you, count, with the gallantry of your nation, no doubt do not consider that, and, as
for me, my conviction of the negative
character of death, makes me quite in-
different to such a risk.'

De Guiscard saw by this time that
Lord Vane would never do for practical
politics.

'I must be off now,' he said, 'for fear of
exciting the suspicion of your people, or
of mine host where I am lodging. Pray
turn the matter over in your mind, and,

above all, get as much information as possible about the king's movements. I will give myself and the cause the pleasure and advantage of conferring with you further in a day or two. You will be at home? Next time I shall send up my name as—say, Johnson—and not look at all as now. One can make a little change go a long way with care. Do not communicate with me otherwise, I beg, my lord; it would not be safe.'

'Very well; but where are you hiding?' asked Lord Vane.

De Guiscard told him.

'That must be a good place,' returned the other, 'for even I scarcely remembered its existence. There is nobody there but an old woman, is there not? But, by the way, don't fall into the Devil's Hole on your way home, the cottage is very near it.'

'I probably shall,' laughed De Guiscard.

'National politeness, my lord ; we Frenchmen all go to the devil, you see, to save him the trouble of fetching us. Good night.'

CHAPTER X.

MEANWHILE Jonathan Swift was working away at Moor Park translating English into Greek and Greek into English, and was making himself so useful that Sir William, diplomatically balancing profit against pleasure, decided against his intuitive dislike of his secretary, and resolved to put up with him as a necessary evil. The two saw each other as little as the exigencies of the Anglo-Greek question would permit of, and Sir William soon found that the more general his instructions the better the work progressed. As for Jonathan, he felt his life would be endurable if he need not be snubbed more than twice a day, and exerted himself to make sure of his post, while at the same time he indulged as freely as he dared when in the baronet's presence in those peculiarities of thought and expression, in paradoxical statements and quaint opinions, which were just such as the sober jog-trot mind of that illustrious mediocrity could not support.

Apart from the interviews with Sir William which this judicious management kept at a minimum, and the smallness of his salary, Jonathan had no external grievance. True, he dined in the buttery with the higher servants, but he had soon come to estimate that pitiful standing insult at what it was worth; and, besides, he preferred infinitely dining with Hestor Johnson to dining alone, not to say with Sir William. Indeed, as the weeks rolled by

and the memory of those awful moments
when he was mindless faded a little, Jonathan began at times to fancy he was happy.
Inspired by the great love he bore the
two dear ones at home, he strove to forget
the cold iron of failure which rankled in
his soul, and to be happy in that best way
—by making others happy. Do not love
him the less, reader, because he often failed to find in love and duty, balm for the
wound of ungratified ambition. He
would have been a god if he had, not a
man. Again and again the passionate
longing to force the world to believe in
him, in spite of all its imbecility and dun-
derheadedness, grew into a mania. There
were other Jonathan Swifts in the world ;
he knew it ; fortunate ones who had been
born with a candlestick to set their light
in. And it was their ' bravoes ' the world
echoed. He would become known to
them, appeal to them. But how ? And

the darkness engulphed him. No words can express what a lion feels to be worried to death by dogs,

Every day, too, he felt, what was worse than the neglect by others of the merits he himself knew were his, the greater evil of a doubt of those merits growing in the inmost recesses of his own heart. Again and again he found himself anxiously wondering whether after all God had given him the stupendous intelligence he had once believed, and then he flew to his Greek translations, or wrote a long letter to Lauriel or his mother, hoping they were moderately comfortable on the pittance he could afford, and abusing Steinkirks.

One morning very early, having exhausted these remedies in vain, and feeling utterly wretched and sick at heart, Jonathan went out into the shrubbery, with an indefinite intention of doing something between breathing the fresh air, writing

an ode on criticism, and drowning himself. To his astonishment Hestor Johnson was there before him.

'How ill you look, Mr. Swift,' she said,
with pretty alarm.

'Do I ?' returned he, brightening up a
good deal by the magic of her presence;
'then I am the very reverse of a gay de-
ceiver—I'm a miserable fact.'

'The truth is,' continued Hestor, seating
herself demurely on a rustic bench as a
throne of judgment—'the truth is, you
work too hard and take too little exercise;
now plead guilty and the court will be
lenient.'

She looked very pretty, with her real
concern peeping through her mock gravity
in fitful flashes, and it seemed more natural to Jonathan to say something about
that than to plead to either count in the
indictment.

'Really, fair judge, you would make the

ugliest wig in creation look like a halo.'

'Order in the court,' she laughed; 're-member, prisoner at the bar, Lord Bacon's essay on judicature, and don't attempt to warp a righteous judgment. Guilty or not guilty?'

'And a sergeant's gown like lilies in all their glory.'

'This is wilful obstruction of the busi-ness of the court,' went on Hestor. 'I shall convict you of contempt, and the sentence is this: You see the cone hill,' pointing with her pretty white finger, 'there is a glorious view from it; it is only five hundred yards from the house to the top, and yet,' solemnly, 'you have never yet ascended it. The court decrees that every morning at ten o'clock, wind and weather——'

'And Sir William Temple,' put in Jona-than—'W. T. and W E T.'

'——permitting, you shall walk, run, or

otherwise progress from the great door to the top of the cone hill and back again.'

'Temper justice with mercy, gracious judge,' said Jonathan, 'and show me the way for the first time, or it may take me as long as Sisyphus.'

'The court consents to the prisoner's petition,' was the merry reply; 'and now the judge is going to pick flowers.'

Another minute, and she had vanished among the shrubs, and it suddenly occurred to Jonathan that he had been quite happy for five consecutive minutes. Then he went back to his translation, and got very little done before ten o'clock came, considering how hard he seemed to be working. Back in the shrubbery again, Jonathan stood waiting for his fair conductress, when a footman brought him a pencil note from Hestor, saying, 'The court is very sorry it cannot go. The prisoner is earnestly requested to undergo the sentence, nevertheless.'

'There is a visitor coming to-day, sir,' said the man, as he handed the note.

'To stay?' asked Jonathan, unconsciously actuated by a desire for the ample leisure to explore the cone hill that would probably follow from Sir William having some antique diplomatist on his hands.

"So I believe, sir,' replied the man.

'Thank you very much,' said Jonathan, seating himself on Hestor's judgment-seat, pulling a copy of his favourite author, Montaigne, out of his pocket, and preparing to enjoy himself for half an hour.

Interest would not waken, however, and in five minutes he was scribbling on the title-page out of the multitude of his heart as follows :—

' How many giant Andes rise,
    In grand confusion hurled,
    More like deep valleys of the skies
    Than mountains of the world !
    Yet which of them, despite their worth,
    A poet's praise e'er knew ?

For mountains cover half the earth,
But poets—they are few !
Then, oh, thou very little hill
(Mere tumult of the plain),
Let proud delight thy bosom fill,
To thus inspire my strain.
Fair, fair, happily fair,
When the sunbeams play with the summer there,
And the thrush and the linnet are learning to sing
From the music of flowerets opening !
Fair, fair, unspeakably fair,
When the winter scowls at his triumph there,
And the birds are flown, and nothing is glad ;
Yea, all the fairer to then be sad.
Fair, fair, serenely fair,   ·
When 'tis neither summer nor winter there,
And the sky seems changing never again.
Oh, how fair to be beautiful then !'

After which, governed by the connection of ideas, he laid down his book and
started for the cone hill at a gawky
trot. Once there, he found that Hestor's
opinion as to the view was quite justified
in fact. 'I wonder which view she prefers,' he thought, gazing leisurely about
him. 'I wish she were here.' And then,

while a flush on the divinely ugly face
showed that Jonathan was a little bit
ashamed of the transposition of his ideas,
'I wish mother and Lauriel were here
too. Miss Johnson has really been very
kind to me ever since I entered this
valley of the shadow of conventionality
and thick-headedness,' ran on his medita-
tions, 'and, on consideration, I have never
done anything to indicate my appreciation of her good Samaritanship. I wonder if she would like some compliment-
ary verses; girls generally do. Those
lines in "Montaigne" would do, with a
tag to them.' So, leaning against a tree,
he proceeded to write the tag.

'But never a hill cared so little as he,
  For he knew I was writing of——

'Bother! "Hestor" won't rhyme. I
must change her name. There, now I
must be off.' And the gawky trot was
put on active service.

Meanwhile, a young man had strolled
up to the seat Jonathan had lately occupied in the shrubbery, and began to
amuse himself with the open copy of
'Montaigne.' It was Henry St. John.
He was dressed extravagantly well; a
little out of the fashion in the sense of
being beyond it; and there was about
him an air of affectation scarcely pronounced enough to be detected in any
overt action, but still undoubtedly there,
in general effect. (I daresay our dear
friends of patchwork vocabulary would
call it a *je ne sais quoi* of conceit, but
then they are in the habit of talking
about 'they don't know what.') That
is what an elderly man would have
noticed. One of his own age, three and
twenty, would have been chiefly struck
by the obvious expression of good-nature
and good-fellowship which played in his
eyes, and which went so far towards

making him the most popular of men wherever he went, while a woman, a real one, not a female man with 'rights' and a university education, would have seen all that, and the fascinating sweetness, the dignity, and the self-confidence too.

Henry St. John was one of the cleverest men of the seventeenth, or, for the matter of that, any other century, and he was perfectly aware of it. I am afraid, reader, you do not love him the better for his self-knowledge; but pray consider. Suppose he had *not* been one of the cleverest men God ever created, suppose, on the other hand, he had been a common-place, humdrum, uninspired British elector, what would have been his choice in introspection according to your creed? Why, to appreciate himself fairly (which is what you object to), or to depreciate himself, and, as a necessary consistent consequence, to apply for admission to a lunatic asylum.

No, no, it is just as sacred a duty to estimate correctly one's abilities as one's want
of them, and nobody doubts *that*. However, I daresay you will like him presently, in spite of his self-appreciation, if not
for it.

Turning over the pages of 'Montaigne,'
his eye chanced to light on the pencilled
verses on the title-page.

'Soho!' he cried, ' "Haunts of the
Muses,"' and stopped short. 'Deep val-
lies of the skies' had arrested his attention. He finished the trifle and re-read
it. Then, pulling out his pencil as a
thought struck him, he wrote underneath
this facetious comment—

> ' The poem is pretty,
> The poet insane,
> To write a " hill " ditty
> Upon a " montaigne." '

Just then Jonathan rounded the corner
(puffing and blowing after his unusual

exertion) to fetch his book before going back to work. St. John divined his intent, and handing the book, said, with a laugh,

'It is yours, I am certain; no one was ever so unfortunate as am I. I can't attempt to purloin a book without being detected in the act, especially if I have first spoiled it by scribbling bad poetry, nay worse, bad puns all over the blank spaces; were it not that I would rather die than borrow even from myself, I would call on the "Montaignes" to fall upon me.'

'Pray don't,' said Jonathan, 'till I am out of the way; and, as to the puns, the only people who don't like them are those who cannot make them. Bravo!' he continued, reading the lines, 'this is of the second order of puns, a "pun with a circumstance."'

'Pardon me,' said St. John, meditatively, 'isn't that a lie?'

'You know best,' laughed Jonathan, 'whether it is altogether Shakespearian or only partly.'

'By the way,' returned St. John, 'I ought to introduce myself and explain why I am trespassing. Excuse me for having forgotten, but it seems to me always so much the most natural thing to do that—however, your humble servant, Henry St. John. Of course the name conveys no impression to your mind as to the owner, and, at any rate, I am not responsible; but, for fear of accidents, allow me to assure you that it is singularly inappropriate.'

'And *your* humble servant, Mr. St. John, Jonathan Swift, local secretary to Sir William Temple; of *me*, that is a full and exhaustive description, for, beyond saying that my name is the best part about me, I can further assure you it is all there is.'

St. John frankly held out his hand.

'You astonish me,' he said. 'I had no notion Sir William had sense enough to appreciate a man of your stamp. How he must bore you! Well, I congratulate Sir William.'

Jonathan's face flushed at these the first words of sympathy he had ever received from any created being save his mother and sister.

'Thank you,' he said, 'for I know you mean that as a compliment; but really when a man, who has succeeded as Sir William has done, does not appreciate anybody (in fact, quite the reverse in my case), where is one bound to suppose the want of sense to lie?'

'Ah, so! he does not then. It did seem marvellous, certainly: and now for your question, let me see—Why, when a man has thrown double sixes ten times running, without having loaded the dice, mind,

should he not have written " Hudibras "
and the " Merchant of Venice "?—I give it
up.'

'Nay,' said Jonathan, with loyal banter,
' surely double sixes had very little to do
with the Triple Alliance.'

' Perhaps not,' replied St. John, ' but
that was paradoxical all through. Fancy
one man composing a triple alliance, yet
that is more than a joke.'

' Well,' replied the secretary, feeling in
honour bound to maintain the credit of his
employer in the eyes of some one who
might be nearly a stranger for aught he
knew, ' it is very kind of him to keep me
here as he does, for he neither likes me
nor in any way believes in me, and I am
an eternal source of irritation to his strong
point, which is—common sense.'

' Yes, that is his strong point, and I
should think you were,' added St. John,
with a merry laugh. Then the two young

men went indoors together, talking and laughing, and a friendship had begun which was never to terminate.

CHAPTER XI.

Henry St. John quite felt he had made a change for the worse when the exigencies of society drove him to leave Jonathan in peace, and go instead to commune with Sir William; but before an hour had elapsed the feeling had deepened to such a degree that he looked forward with lively dread to the dinner time. Cut-and-dry politics had been talked out, so had cut-and-dry art, literature, and theology. What was to be done at dinner? Both the old man and the young one could talk, and each very well, but it was quite beyond them to talk to each other.

Poor St. John, who was never satisfied with knowledge, had vainly endeavoured to extract real information from the veteran diplomatist on those subjects with which he was best acquainted, especially the Continental History of England during the last few years of Charles II., and had very soon stopped in despair. There is a living English statesman who is probably the most overrated man in all this overrated age. Some people compare him to Burke —God help thee, Edmund, truly thy pearls are cast before swine!—but there is a remnant left in Israel who know better. Well, this statesman talks eternally about the Crimean War, and knows every fact in history but one, namely, that the beings it concerns are *men*. That fact Sir William Temple had not mastered either, and so the future Viscount Bolingbroke very soon tired of dummy substitutes. Come to a dead-lock, Sir William barked back to the cause of his young friend's visit, and they set to work to perpetrate the transparent fraud on each other of talking the whole thing over again.

'Your father and I were always such very good friends, Mr. St. John, that I should be only too glad to do anything in my power to oblige his son or even his son's friend, but of course it is much more easy to do the former than the latter. You see I can myself *do* nothing now-a-days. The limit of my tether is asking some one else to do something, and you can conceive how much the force of any such application varies according to the personal favour which the granting of it would seem to confer on myself, and *that* of course depends exclusively on my relationship to the person for whom I ask consideration.'

'Quite so, Sir William,' answered the

young man, eagerly grasping the renewed
opportunity of pleading for his friend,
'but I imagined that though, of course,
you could not ask much for one in whom
you had no direct interest, still you could
ask something ; and pray remember that a
very little would be a great deal to him.
A clerkship in the War office, Home office,
any office would at least give poor Matthew Prior an opportunity of showing what
he is worth, would give him more spare
time, and, above all, would raise him out
of the unspeakably soul-degrading position
of common pot-boy in a common inn.'

'Well, I will think about it,' replied Sir
William, 'but do not fancy you have set
me an easy task. Remember that though
there are a good many clerkships, there
are ten times as many people crowding to
fill them, and probably as many patrons,
each pushing his best, and each just as
omnipotent as you seem to fancy me to be.

Tell me, now, how did you come across this Bacchanalian Muse.'

'Well, Sir William, I will be frank and tell you exactly how, for though it does not redound to my credit still it does to that of poor Matt, and, besides, I know that with your enormous experience of human nature you don't expect young men to be young women.' Sir William bowed at the compliment, and St. John went on. 'Matt, so far as he knows, has only got one relative in the world, his uncle, James Prior, who keeps a tavern in Cheapside, and sells, by the way, some very excellent claret. It is a quiet house, so I often dine there with a friend when business calls me up to town.'

'Or pleasure?' queried Sir William.

'Well, yes, or pleasure,' answered St. John. 'One evening as I walked down Cheapside on my way to the tavern, in company with a man, who shall be nameless, because of ensuing circumstances, we met as we neared the door a remarkably pretty girl. She was shabbily dressed, but there was an air of quiet dignity about her which stamped her in my eyes as a lady at once, whether rich or poor. She seemed desirous to escape observation, and was walking hurriedly along looking at no one. The man I was with saw her coming and pointed her out to me. He was a thoroughly vulgar fellow with not one refined feeling from head to foot. "A pretty baggage," he said. His tone annoyed me. "She is a perfect lady," I returned, shortly. "Bet you a hundred guineas she's not," he replied, "and toss you who runs the risk of kissing her as proof." Thoroughly savage, I took the bet, and lost the toss before giving myself a moment to reflect on the brutality of my conduct, and just as she was passing Prior's tavern, I stepped up and kissed her. All

I had time to see was, that she turned a ghostly white, and stood quite still, trembling from head to foot, for the next instant Matthew Prior had felled me by a blow from his fist. I was up again in an instant, and——'

'Ran him through the body, I suppose; a mercy it was not mortal,' put in Sir William.

'Oh, no,' said St. John, 'I had come to my senses as quickly as I went out of them; so of course I shook hands with him, and thanked him for giving me just what I deserved. The same evening I fought my " friend " (having Matt for my second) for insulting the lady.'

'But you were equally guilty,' said Sir William, not a little amazed.

'True,' was the reply, 'and we ran equal risk. It was one of the few duels, of which the result could not be unjust, and to be short, I put his arm in a sling for six weeks, my broken head lasting about the same time.'

'It was courageous, certainly, for a man in the position of Mr. Prior to do such a thing,' said Sir William; 'if you *had* run him through, nothing would have been done to you after such provocation. It was certainly a terrible risk. But though you don't seem to see it in that light, my dear St. John, your part in the transaction was more noble by far. You are a worthy son of your father, sir, and though I have heard a great deal about your follies, and your worse than follies, I am very glad to see you at Moor Park; and, if I can do anything for your chivairous friend, rely upon me I shall do it.'

After which destruction of the barriers of diplomatic reserve, Sir William felt scarcely comfortable. 'You run too much after pretty faces,' he remarked at length. 'Take care, for the sake of the

great name you bear. You must sober
down, get married, go into Parliament, to
be able to say you have sat there : there is
no necessity to do any work——'

'There is nothing would please me better than a seat in the Commons house,'
returned the young man, 'but as to getting married—hm !——Who, Sir William,
in a more or less remote connection with
that subject, is the very pretty girl I saw
this morning in the garden?'

The statesman rose, and sauntered to
the window.

'In the garden? Where?'

'She is the last person whose latitude
and longitude need specification,' said St.
John, with a laugh. 'She makes them,
she is her own 'sun. You cannot have
seen her if you do not know her.'

'If she was dark,' said Sir William,
from the shelter of the window recess,
while feelings agitated him of which his

companion never dreamt, 'it was probably Hestor Johnson whom you saw.'

'Very well, I adore Hestor Johnson,' answered St. John : 'but who is she?'

'The orphan of my late steward,' replied the other. 'He was my good servant for many years, and, as I have no means of recompensing him personally, I do all in my power for his daughter. She lives here, doing nothing but amusing herself with music and books, or as she pleases. So it has been for years. I must look after her better now, however. Let me see, she is sixteen, I think; it is scarcely fair to leave her so entirely to her own devices now. I shall send her away from Moor Park in charge of some elderly dame or other. If not, she will probably marry a footman!'

'Why not?' asked St. John, somewhat astonished.

Sir William had turned towards the

window again, and seemed to be observing something very intently as he answered,

'Oh, merely because I should be glad to see her more comfortably settled for her father's sake.'

'Well, Sir William,' laughed St. John, 'I can only say that either that steward was an abnormally good steward, or else you are an abnormally good master.'

Then that subject dropped too, and the elder man looked anxious, the young one a little bored.

'I hope,' presently remarked the visitor, 'that my sudden arrival has not greatly inconvenienced you in any way. Some one may be going to dine with you on political business, or a hundred things. Pray, don't let me stand in your way, whatever happens.'

'No, I am quite alone,' was the reply, 'as, indeed, I nearly invariably am.' Poor St. John drew a mental sigh. It was, then, as he had feared, a dual dinner that he saw before him. 'Your company will be quite an agreeable change, I assure you.'

The young man believed, however, that he bored his distinguished friend, and knew that his distinguished friend bored him, and very naturally Jonathan Swift occurred to him as a prospective remedy. While he was wondering how to compass his object, and obtain an invitation for Lazarus to the rich man's table, Sir William was called away, and St. John took the opportunity of retreating to the shrubbery, conventionality permitting. Hestor Johnson was there when he entered, but the instant she saw him she turned to go away, as in steward-daughter bound. He stopped her, however, with the easy affability of a superior.

'Pray, do not let me disturb you, Miss Johnson; we are very nearly related:

you are Johns'n and I am St. John.'

'It makes a good deal of difference evidently,' was the quietly vindictive reply, 'or I also would probably have had the revelation you have been so obviously vouchsafed on the subject of manners.'

Poor St. John was aghast.

'Pray, forgive me,' he cried. 'I never can apologise enough, but I took you to be a Miss Johnson about whom Sir William Temple had just been speaking, and addressed you in the tone which would have been suitable for her, though how unsuitable for you, heaven knows.'

Hestor laughed a malicious little laugh.

'Then, I presume, Sir William has the honour of your acquaintance, possibly you are nearly related.'

'Don't be cruel, I beseech you,' cried St. John. 'I did not mean to be rude.'

'Never mind, I will take the will for the deed,' answered Hestor.

'Now then,' he said, 'I feel much more like St. Sebastian than St. John—utterly riddled—so please let me stay and hear you talk about somebody else; it would do me good. May I?'

She looked at him with clear, impassive eyes, her revenge not yet exhausted.

'Certainly; but I don't know the angel Gabriel, and of course he comes next —after you.'

'Well, it's lucky for the angel Gabriel that he never mistook you for Miss Johnson,' said St. John; 'but, if I were he, I would risk all for the sake of making your acquaintance.'

'He being Personius to your Alexander?'

'I am a friendless stranger, miss— madam, and, if you destroy me, it is fair to warn you that the carcass will probably be left on your hands.'

Hestor smiled, and St. John discovered,

to his amazement, that a created being could be more beautiful than Hestor severe.

'Don't be alarmed,' she said. 'I will leave you life enough to enable you to go away.'

'Meanwhile,' he answered, as a leading question—for he was dying with anxiety to know who this fair creature was—'you have before you the mortal remains of Henry St. John, inanimate, save by a sense of insignificance.'

She did not offer to enlighten him, however, for she keenly enjoyed making him understand what a steward's daughter might be, and that would come best as a disclosure. So she only assumed an unutterably pretty air of mocking patronage, and said, soothingly,

'Never mind, one sense is much more than most people have.'

'Stay,' he interposed, 'or you will deprive me of it. Change the subject while there is time; talk about—about—about Mr. Swift; you know him.' St. John had pitched, in his haste to escape from his tormentor, upon the first human being who occurred to him and could be probably made to serve the purpose. He fancied that just the very faintest additional colour came into the fair cheeks before him when he said it, and added instantly, with the tact which was part of his nature, ' Or the garden, the flowers, anything.'

Hestor saw the little addition, and, divining its object, felt grateful to the author of it, and of course, just because of that, she refused to leave Jonathan the prey of silence.

' Mr. Swift? Certainly. Well, I like Mr. Swift very much; don't you ?'

' Immensely,' answered St. John. ' But, to be quite frank, I only met him here for ten minutes or so—half an hour, perhaps—and quite by accident, this very morning.'

'Ah! Of course you like him, everybody must like him; but you don't know him. Half an hour—no. I don't know him. He has only been here a few weeks. If one studied Mr. Swift carefully every day for forty years, one might stand a dim indistinct chance of really understanding him. If he succeed, as he deserves to do, he is capable of leaving something behind him which will enable the whole world to understand him two hundred years hence better than they will while he lives— through an interpreter, of course—I mean it will give him a chance of having an interpreter who *feels with him,* without which nobody will ever comprehend Jonathan Swift, any more than without such sympathy one can comprehend the Bible.'

'Every day for forty years! Then the sooner I begin the better. Do you know whether he will dine with us this evening? And shall I begin at his head or his feet?'

'Firstly, yes,' she said; 'secondly, I daresay, though, as a rule, no; and thirdly, I strongly recommend you to begin with his feet, because then you may some day get to his head, whereas, *vice versâ*, you will never get to his feet.'

'What, not in forty years!'

'Ignoring the sneer—no, don't protest—would you like to begin it this evening?'

'Well, really,' said St. John, 'if you are going to do us the unspeakable honour of gracing Sir William's table, I am too lost in rapture to desire any further felicity.'

'Oh, dear me, how clumsy! I!—certainly not; I dine in the buttery. Good-bye for the present.' And, with a smile of mischievous delight at the look of blank amazement on the face of her mystified auditor, she glided away through the bushes.

CHAPTER XII.

LORD BACON says, 'Some have been so curious as to note that the times when the stroke or percussion of an envious eye doth most hurt are when the party envied is beheld in glory or triumph, for that sets an edge upon envy; and besides, at such times, the spirits of the person envied do come forth most into the outward parts, and so meet the blow.' This may be true or it may not; I cannot say. The nineteenth century has given in. To get at causes, properly so called (barring altogether the first cause, for the nineteenth century fancies it understands that), it scorns to make an effort. In every sense of the word, the nineteenth century lives for effect. Doctors publish in the *Times* that they do not aim at abolishing the disease, but at curing the patient, or, in other words, their ideal is a guinea a visit. Lawyers carefully avoid deciding *anything* but just the point necessary to wrong somebody; but then their ideal is—thank God, I do not know! Artists: there is Sir Noel Paton in the nineteenth century, before whom I bow down and worship, but the Lord deliver us from rubbish and shams, and Ruskin and Turner, women peeling potatoes, and 'notes in green.' I am not in the habit, reader, of troubling you with many digressions, so pray excuse this one. It was inspired by this reflection that fortune always dealt its hardest blows to Jonathan Swift just when, according to Lord Bacon's hypothesis, he was least prepared to resist them.

To proceed, however. Monsieur de Guiscard felt quite certain, after having slept over it, that all he should gain by having introduced himself to Lord Vane was information. His assistance was clearly worse than useless; because it might, or it might not—just according to what appeared at the last moment to the noble peer the most conclusive reason—be relied on. The position was, however, a difficult one. Not even the logical owner of Vane Castle would have submitted to being proved untrustworthy, let the premisses be ever so good. In that case, the chances are that he would have discovered some irrefragable reason for paying those who were so injudiciously syllogistic in the coin of their suspicion. Clearly Lord Vane must be concerned in some plot, if only to keep him quiet, and to recompense him for the information he was to procure.

So thought Monsieur de Guiscard, and to him the solution was quite obvious. Apart from the ten commandments, a believed lie is better than truth ; for it serves the same purpose and provides as well the intellectual exercise involved in sticking to it ; it was by the light of this axiom, in which he implicitly believed, not being troubled at all by the ten commandments, that Monsieur de Guiscard saw the way out of the difficulty. But then, though nothing was easier than to construct a dummy plot, it was a more serious question how to carry out the real one single-handed.

Over this difficult question Monsieur de Guiscard thought long and painfully. One scheme after another flitted, bat-like, through his mind, only to disappear amid the clouds of obvious impracticability. A conspirator who has no earthly object in view but his own advantage, is a much more dangerous man than is he who, inspired by a passionate faith in somebody or something, struggles for the benefit of him or it. The cause which over-shadows self, overshadows difficulties, and difficulties unseen are difficulties doubled. There was no fear of any such contingency with Monsieur de Guiscard, however. It could not serve his purpose to die in the execution of the deed he had to do ; so, be-sides seeing his way to success, he had to see his way to safety. Now, reader, what would you have done had you been he, that is to say had you been a man of des-perate fortunes, with only one tender human oasis in a life of shame and crime, only one tender human longing to palliate the remnant that was left, and only one chance of realizing that longing ? Pray, con-sider your answer when you read what Monsieur de Guiscard did. It arose thus.

Some weeks had elapsed since the storm

bore its fateful burden to Mrs. Swift's door, and Monsieur de Guiscard imagined it would be wise to test the feeling of his hostess as to his continued sojourn. True, he contributed handsomely to the joint expenses. He had made a point of that.

'You grant me shelter,' he had said, 'you run a great personal risk for me. I consent to that because in my weakness, my helplessness, I must, or I must perish; but to be a burden to you unnecessarily, and while I can well afford to support my-self, Mrs. Swift, never!'

And besides he had made himself ex-ceedingly pleasant. So agreeable, indeed, that a very few days had changed the mo-tive for giving him sanctuary from human-ity to friendship.

Well, one day, after having spent the morning in vain cogitations, and having got no further than a vague idea that he could mine under the high road and blow

King William to eternity, *if* anyone would light the match, but that to do so alone, undefended, was certain death, the count went down stairs to join Mrs. Swift and Lauriel at dinner.

On such occasions, conversation was always preceded by a few words of inquiry on the part of the gentleman as to news of his persecutors, and an expression of hearty sympathy and gratitude on that of the ladies for their visitor's continued safety. This time, however, De Guiscard changed its even tenor. With an air in which regret, concern and thanksgiving were admirably blended, he walked up to Mrs. Swift, and, raising her hand to his lips, said, with a most natural artificial effort,

' My dear Mrs. Swift, the time has come for me to go. I can very probably succeed now in eluding detection. The search for me must have relaxed. I will not attempt to thank you for your kindness. It would be in vain. But God knows the depth of my gratitude, and what I would do, not in repayment, but in loving service, if I had it in my power. And you, Miss Swift, who have been a very angel of light to a broken-down, ruined, refugee French soldier of fortune, God reward you too.'

Lauriel had turned very pale, and Monsieur de Guiscard saw it.

'You do nothing of the kind,' put in Mrs. Swift, with more energy than was usual to her; 'to go yet would be to court destruction. Your enemies are implacable; this delay in arresting you will merely have whetted their appetite for revenge. No, Monsieur de Guiscard, go you must not. I should never forgive myself if I allowed you to run so awful a risk without doing everything in my power to deter you. Don't you think so, Lauriel?'

'Certainly, mamma.'

'Well, really,' said the count, 'you have half frightened me out of my resolution.'

'I sincerely trust I have,' went on Mrs. Swift; 'and, moreover, I do not for one moment believe that you yourself really consider it safe to go. The fact is, that rather than be, as you imagine, in our way, and inflict on us more of your society than you conceive we can support, you will run the risk of dying the death of a felon. Now, on your word, Monsieur de Guiscard, is not that so?'

'Well, beyond all question, I must be an incredible nuisance, of course; but, altogether apart from that——'

'There is nothing whatever apart from that. Promise me, I pray, that you will reconsider your determination.'

'Then I surrender,' answered the count, 'to your infinite goodness, and will bore you a little while longer.'

A consummate actor, Monsieur de Guiscard never forgot his character. In all his efforts to amuse his hostesses and to gain that regard which would doubly ensure the safety of his concealment, he had always contrived to mix enough appearance of the struggle it cost him to be gay, to maintain at once his *rôle*, and to lend an additional value to his good nature. It was sometimes of course only too easy for him to appear miserable, but against *that* he fought. It was too awful to be so unutterably miserable as that.

At dinner on the day of the conversation we have recited, Monsieur de Guiscard was, however, in exuberant spirits, and he could not help showing it. In Lauriel's pale face he had received a very revelation. She was more than sorry when he said he must go, and worse than afraid. Yet he had paid her no special attention, nor attempted in any way to gain her affection. Nevertheless, she cared for him, clearly, very much. And, as he thought so, he suddenly heard across the time, 'Kiss me, Henri, before I go away for ever,' and he shuddered. 'But your love has been blighted, why not another?' whispered the fiend within him, and his soul echoed, 'Why not?' Then, loving thus for nothing, what would she love for love, he thought? What would she not *do* for it? Ay, what would she not risk for it? What was there women had not risked, dared, defied, for love? The thought set his whole being aglow. The way was clear now.

Lauriel was very silent during dinner: unusually so. She generally took the brunt of the conversation upon herself, partly to save her mother from fatigue and partly because she felt it a duty to cheer and divert poor Monsieur de Guis-card as well as might be, a task for which

Mrs. Swift was sadly unfit. It was very difficult for *her* to be gay. The count's fit of exuberant, irrepressible spirits was very opportune, therefore. Lauriel sheltered behind it, so to speak, smiled mechanically at the jokes she scarcely heard, and thought. She hardly knew what it meant that feeling of dull sorrow which had flooded her soul when this acquaintance of a few weeks had said, 'I must go.' Yet it had been a very real pain, and a very deep one.

Poor little Lauriel! And the relief, the joy, quiet, intense, when he had said he would stay a little longer, only temper-ed by the prospect, unthought of before, that it was only a little longer. It was a relief to her when the short repast was over, and she could go upstairs to have a penitent cry over the truth slowly dawn-ing upon her. How sweet, how foolish, how irrevocable. Presently she came downstairs again feeling very happily miserable, and was astonished to find Monsieur de Guiscard evidently waiting for her.

' I am so glad you have come,' he said, ' I want to ask a favour.'

He spoke in a tender tone she had never heard inspire his voice before, yet she had often noticed how sweet and gentle that voice was. I daresay that as a matter-of-fact it was no whit changed from its ordinary, but—

> ' There is a power in Love
> Beyond what mortals dream of. He alone
> Is not a debtor to the power of sense,
> A slave to five poor miserable means
> Of working out his great Supremacy.
> No! he has agents we know nothing of,
> Subtle as ether, strong as Destiny,
> Connecting soul with soul.'

' Yes ?'

The count noticed the new-found timidity of her glance.

'Yes, I want you to take me to see the waterfall at the Devil's Hole. It is quite near this, is it not? Yet I have never chanced to see it all these weeks.'

'Oh, no, Monsieur de Guiscard, it would not be safe. It is barely dusk yet. You are growing rash and reckless. Remember the risk you run. Oh, no, no, this will never do.'

'Indeed, yes,' he pleaded. 'It rained all this morning, and is cloudy still. No one will trouble to walk up from the village on a day like this, and there is nobody nearer. I have really been more careful than necessity required. I don't believe ten people come here in as many years. Do *please*. The walk would be such a treat. My nocturnal expeditions are a poor substitute for strolls by daylight—and with you.'

She walked to the door and looked out, hesitating.

'Certainly it is a very, very little way : stay, I will run and see if any denizens of the dreary waste are about.'

A few minutes, and she had returned, prettily breathless, with heightened colour and eyes full of happiness.

'Yes, you may come, there is no one near; and the trees shade the Hole so well, one cannot be seen, once one is there, you know.'

So they went, the dark line and the golden mingling ever more surely. Alas ! brother, brother,—the dream, alas ! the dream !

Let us leave them sitting on a ledge of rock looking down into the deep black water ; for, worse luck, it is necessary that I should describe to you the Devil's Hole. Exactly, I mean, like a geologist, or an auctioneer, or a modern poet.

About two hundred yards from the door of Mrs. Swift's cottage, a limestone ridge rose abruptly, rearing a vertical face of some twenty feet high, sheer out of the plain. Apparently the result of a fault in the formation, which had allowed a partial subsidence to take place, it was traversed obliquely by another fault which cut a narrow gorge through the cliff, but which everywhere else was filled by the accumulations of centuries, and was indistinguishable from the surrounding surface. Thickly studded by trees and extensive patches of underwood as the whole country was, the little gorge was not readily to be found by a stranger, and might even be missed by one who knew it well. Through it was the way to the Devil's Hole. For, far away down below the surface, a subterranean river had eaten its way along the fault, coming no one knew whence, and going no one knew whither. But a little way further on a vast hole yawned black and sullen, and down its steep, rocky sides one could look and see a mighty torrent rushing in with throbs, like the beat of a human pulse, and fall, fall, falling, till the eye refused to follow and the mind to think. A terrible place, truly, but Lauriel does not think so to-day. Listen, they have sat long and are coming away at last, her hand held fast in his.

'I used to be frightened of the waterfall, oh, so frightened; I fancied that somehow it was my fate, and shrank from it (Jonathan used to say so, half in jest, half in earnest) and I could not bear to hear its rumbling, those pulses seemed always to say, "Come, Stephanie, come, Stephanie, come." Jonathan heard it too—that is why he began to call me Lauriel; it isn't my real name, you know. But now! oh, how I love it. And I have gone to it, haven't I, and how kind it has been to me; we will both of us love it, always, always, won't we—Henri?'

Then he stooped and kissed her forehead. May God forgive him, for I never can.

CHAPTER XIII.

However it came about, it did come about that Henry St. John was not ·the only guest Sir William Temple entertained at the dinner the former had so much dreaded. Jonathan Swift was there too. He had been invited by a characteristic note.

'Dear Mr. Swift,

  'If you are not otherwise engaged, I shall be glad if you will be my guest at dinner this evening.

   'Yours faithfully.'

'Be my guest,' was the neat way in

which Sir William conveyed, to one whom he knew very well would understand a hint, the idea that neither Jonathan nor anybody else was, while at his table, looked upon by him as other than a gentleman and an equal.

As for Jonathan, he would very much have preferred not to go. Of all the things which he detested the one he hated most utterly was being in society which had a right to esteem itself as his superior. ' Were I acknowledged,' he would say, ' as I shall be if I have time, then I would mix, and willingly, with men whose accidents of birth and fortune are so much beyond mine, as my accident of intelligence is beyond theirs. Meantime, no.'

And although he was well aware that Sir William would treat him precisely as he would treat anybody else, and listen attentively to his opinions, defer courteously to his judgments, and applaud his wit quite as agreeably as though he were dealing with a ducal guest instead of an amanuensis one, still, he also knew that that was because Sir William was a gentleman, and not because his secretary was Jonathan Swift. It would be deference to good breeding, not deference to him. I think Jonathan Swift was right. Nothing is more usual than to see men, ay, and women, too, crawling, creeping, wriggling into society, which is unanimous in regarding them, when it deigns to do so at all, with passive contempt, and then, heaven help them, they think themselves dignified by the contact. After all, I daresay they are; at any rate, it cannot possibly degrade them.

Before making up his mind, however, to refuse, he had gone to consult, as was becoming usual for him, Hestor Johnson, and she had insisted so strongly on how unwise it would be to do so, as to carry her point. So Jonathan dined with Sir William Temple for the first time in his life.

Dinner passed off very pleasantly. Sir William did just talking enough to make the young men talk, throwing in occasionally an anecdote culled from a long experience. St. John chattered away interminably, leaving nobody time to consider what a miracle it was he never seemed to talk too much; while Jonathan, when the strange feeling of his new position wore off, enjoyed himself immensely. Presently, through the medium of a discussion on Shakespeare, somebody reached the mazy question of different types of character.

' Ah,' said Sir William, ' that is a subject which only experience can give an acquaintance with. To get a character out of a book is an impossibility. You can get something, a hint that Tom was

wicked, Dick worse, and Harry worst of
all, but that is no more a "character"
than the colour of the eyes is a portrait.
The whole character is the whole man.
As ambassador at the Hague, I once met a
man who interested me very much. I
will tell you about him, if you won't be
bored, as a sample of what I mean. It
won't lay open to you the individual's
character, but it will convey some idea of
the complications involved in such a study.
Silly people talk about the fidelity of ro-
mances to nature, when, as they say, each
action in these is the necessary outcome
of a certain character face to face with a
certain circumstance. But of course, in
nature, character *is* circumstance, and that
is all we can concern ourselves with; for
out of nature, or more correctly, above it,
character is the Grace of God and passes
knowledge. Would you like to hear of
my French friend as the best contribution

I can offer to the entertainment, and for which I fear, so far, I have done very little—a slight headache, gentlemen, so pray excuse my not having been a good host.'

Being pressed to favour his guests with the story, Sir William recounted a dark tale of a ruined life, blurred, disfigured, almost blotted out by crime, and vice, and wretchedness, yet strangely lit now and then by unexpected goodnesses.

'By the way, Sir William,' St. John said, when he concluded, 'you have never mentioned the fellow's name.'

'True. He was a marquis (though he never used the title) as well as an abbé. He generally called himself the Count de Guiscard.'

Jonathan started.

'Was he,' he said,—'but stay, it is some years since you saw him. Just before I left home to come here a distinguished looking man, calling himself Monsieur de Guiscard, came to the cottage to seek shelter from a terrific storm which was raging. He was French beyond all question, tall, good-looking, and his age might be anything. It could scarcely have been he, however, or he would have given a false name.'

'Nay,' said Sir William, 'I am not at all sure of that. The fellow is consummate liar enough to know the absurdity of telling a useless lie. The odds were millions to one against your having ever heard his name. Had he given another, complications might just as readily have arisen out of it, as from his own. At any rate, I will mention the matter in writing to London. Do you know where he is now, or where he was going?'

As Jonathan said 'No,' how little he imagined what the conversation that so closed would bring forth.

There was still more involved in that evening's entertainment of infinite consequence to our hero as the reader will see. The question of Triennial Parliaments, being the great political question of the day, of course came up for discussion in good time, and Sir William, who was a man of extensive information and sound common sense, was much struck with the complete grasp Jonathan seemed to have of the constitutional questions involved. He seemed to possess a perfect appreciation of the statesmanship of the issue, as opposed to the politics of it, which amazed the professional diplomatist. Sometimes Jonathan could not resist a startling paradoxical expression of what was, after all, sound sense, which irritated Sir William's somewhat common-place preferences, but there was enough for all that of the kind of talent he *could* appreciate to raise his secretary very much indeed in his estimation.

It was, on the other hand, the sparks which St. John looked for when he remembered the unknown beauty's warning, and he rejoiced to see that, with all his sense, Jonathan preferred a good thing to a defensible position.

'Absolute monarchy is tyranny, but absolute democracy is tyranny and anarchy both,' said St. John, whose views were in a minority.

'Yes, tyranny *over* anarchy,' was the reply.

'Nay, all revelation and history contradict that.'

'Both of them can't. They are diametrically opposite. Revelation is, "God is Love," History, "man isn't."'

It so chanced that a London post arrived as they were chatting, and as it brought some very important dispatches

from court for Sir William, he excused
himself, for fear an immediate reply
might be required, and retired to the
library to read them.   Left alone, the
young men had a long and earnest conversation, some of which, reader, please
excuse my recording.   I want you to
get a glimpse of the man as he really
was, before what was coming, came.

'Is that really your reading of history?'
asked St. John.   'Do you see nothing
less diabolical than that in all the re-
cords of all the ages; or to your mind,
in good earnest, would "Man is Hate"
be a fair, impartial epitaph on that race
which was once created in God's own
image?'

'No,'—mark it, reader.   'No.   I see
what is coming.   You will tell me I
would rather libel my species than miss
the occasion for a joke.   Still, no, that
is not my reading of history, I do *not*

find that "Man is Hate." That would involve his being hateful, and I don't think he is. He is very generally stupid, but not by any manner of means offensive or obnoxious. I have been forced to despise the intellectual capacities of a great many people both in history and experience, but, do you know, I hardly believe in villainy.'

'Marvellous!' answered St. John. 'You are not so much of a misanthrope as am I —in fact, it was only the exclusiveness, the grasp of your epigram, that I objected to. ALL men are not hate, and all men are not hateful, but a very great many are —most, in fact. So much as that appears in the terms of ordinary conversation. Somebody by a little inconvenience saves from ruin a dear friend, perhaps a relative, and everybody else says, "What self-sacrifice!" They can't conceive of its being the least self-sacrificing thing he could have done. And generosity, giving something away, has come to be synonymous with what, rightly considered, is the colossal satisfaction of forgiving an injury. Is not that hateful?'

'Why, no,' answered Jonathan. 'I really do not think so. Such clerical errors reflect the stupidity of the race, not its viciousness. To be frank, too, I am sorry I agree with you even as far as I do. Once I would have felt more at my ease in maintaining the cause of mankind as being very little lower than the angels; but I have met with a good deal of trouble, we have had a good deal at home, and it is difficult to be enthusiastic over a race which seems eternally to ill-treat all that is nearest and dearest to one.'

St. John looked curiously at his new friend.

'Pardon me, Mr. Swift,' he said; 'you think the world only stupid because it only does not appreciate you—you are right; but you will hate it when it wrongs you too.'

'Then I pray God it never may, for it would be a terrible thing and a devilish to hate, hate, hate. So far am I from that at present, at least,' he added, with a smile, 'that my ambition is to take holy orders, and do, as a clergyman, all the good I can to my fellow-creatures. From *that* point of view I don't think the buffets of an entire generation could make me hate a single individual. One is forced to remember always that the greatest evil is only misdirected good, and that men, truly images of God, might possibly be evolved by changes, only He knows how slight, from natures the vilest, meanest, and most despicable. Besides, whatever one is, lay or clerical, how could one ever be so un-just as to bear an antipathy to an entire race, and that one's own, because of the injustice, perfidy, wickedness, cruelty, what you will, of a few?—for, after all, it is only at the hands of a few that any man can suffer.'

'You forget,' replied St. John, 'you are a man too, and of like passions with themselves. That would be the why and wherefore, if the test ever came (as I do hope most devoutly it never may) to you or to me. There is one great advantage I have over many people,' he added, changing his tone, 'for, however I may come to hate mankind if they drive me to it, I shall never swerve from adoring the ladies. By the way, that reminds me I had an adventure in the shrubbery this morning.'

Jonathan began to feel vaguely uncomfortable.

'You did!' he cried. 'Uncommonly clever of you, I'm sure. Nobody else ever succeeded in penetrating the prose of Moor Park before. Well, what was it?'

'More correctly, what was *she?* I don't know—do you? This is the description— heaven on earth garnished with Chili vinegar.'

Jonathan smiled.

'That would be a bad-tempered defini- tion of Miss Johnson; but it couldn't have been she; she is too reserved—it might appear like pride to a stranger—to have spoken to you.'

'No, it was not Miss Johnson. I thought it was, and addressed her as one would a person in her position. Oh, dear me, I shall never forget it!'

Jonathan was disgusted to feel he was quite glad of poor St. John's misfortunes, and that it was hard work to even ap- pear sympathetic; but when his friend had told the whole story he knew it was Hestor. However, the twinge of jealousy and the natural elation at the opinion she had expressed about himself were swallowed up in amazement. 'What is the mystery underlying this?' he thought. 'Can the way in which her wish appears to be law be merely coincidence? Or why, in the name of all that is occult, does Sir William do me the incredible honour of asking me to dinner, simply because she appears to have wished it?'

CHAPTER XIV.

NEXT morning Jonathan Swift awoke in the best of spirits. The events of the day before had cheered him up wonderfully. Hope had sprung afresh in his heart. Perhaps things would come right some day. It was just possible that he might succeed, after all; that the world would cease to trample on him; that his talents might be recognized, and his glorious ambition to be great, and to be greatly good, be reached. The approbation of one young man of four and twenty may seem a slight enough peg on which to hang such high anticipations, but it was the first masculine encouragement Jonathan had ever known, and he valued it proportionately. Besides, St. John's was more than an individual opinion, it was a power. The days of "noble authors and distinguished critics" were not then over.

'Let but a lord confess the happy lines,
  How the sense brightens, how the wit refines!'

wrote Pope a good while later. And, though St. John was not in that happy position himself, his high connections and his intimate relations with many of the leaders of wit and fashion, made his good word almost as valuable as though he were. Speaking of Matthew Prior the night before to Jonathan, he said, 'If Sir William cannot do anything for him, I shall go to the Earl of Dorset.' Fancy what a prospect was there for a poor dejected author who had never got be-

yond the circle of publishers and critics,
and who had to rely upon sheer happy-
go-lucky for the felicity of a single man
of intelligence happening to ever see his
book at all. And a very poor chance
that is. Everybody worth mentioning,
from Jonathan Swift to Thomas Carlyle,
can vouch for it.

So, I repeat, Jonathan awoke that morning in the best of spirits. So good were
they that he screwed up his courage to
do a thing which he had not dared to
do since the last failure—he dared to
write. He went to a drawer, unlocked
it, and took out his once dearly-beloved
'Tale of a Tub,' and began to glance
approvingly over the pages. Presently,
some quaint notions came to him, as was
their wont, and he decided to add them
to the tale. Fearing, however, to be disturbed if he remained in his room, and
being quite decided that the inspiration

was too good to be lost, he bethought
him of a nook in the garden where he
often sat, and took his writing materials
thither.   A very pleasant nook it was,
and one where he was quite safe from
interruption.   He had found it by chance
one day while in pursuit of a poor wounded raven, whose broken wing he thought
it might be possible to set.   It was in
the heart of a gigantic laurel which grew
close by the pathway.   All round it appeared one solid mass of foliage, black
and impenetrable, but some frost, or accident of years before, had killed the great
central trunk, and it had been sawn off
at a very convenient height, as Jonathan observed, for a table, while several
branches growing out from it formed a
fair, natural substitute for an arm-chair.

Comfortably settled there, Jonathan
began to write the ' digression concerning
critics.'   Buried in his work, he got as

far as the 'third and noblest sort of critics,' explaining how 'every true critic is a hero born, descending in a direct line from a celestial stem by Momus and Hybris, who begat Zoilus, who begat Tigellius, who begat Etcetera the elder, who begat Bentley, and Rhymer, and Wotton, and Perrault, and Dennis, who begat Etcetera the younger,' when he became conscious of a giddiness and faintness gradually stealing over him.   He tried to rise, but was forced by the feeling of dull helplessness to sit down again, and, the languour increasing rapidly, in a very few minutes he was in a dead faint.   How long he lay unconscious propped by the kindly branches of the laurel, he never knew. Sense came back very, very slowly, and all recollection blotted out for the time of where he was and why; he fancied that he heard in a dream Sir William Temple talking to Hester Johnson very softly and tenderly thus:

'How sorry I am, what my regret is, no one knows, certainly, poor child, *you* do not. The ill done cannot be undone, but, Hestor, it may be intensified, and it is against that I am so anxious to guard, and yet, without exposure, how can I? So far is certain, that I have allowed you to stay here too long. While you were a child it did not matter. It could attract no attention, invite no questioning that the orphan of my steward should shelter beneath my roof; but now— Besides, it is not good for you. The society into which you are forced for the sake of appearances, the subterfuges you are obliged to practise, the treatment you receive——'

'You are very good, very good indeed; pray don't think of those things. Do you think it better I should go away? Of course I will if you wish it, if it is necessary for the sake of appearances; but don't send me for my own sake. I am very happy here, and many things that would annoy you very much don't trouble me at all. You see I have been accustomed to the society I live in all my life. It does not jar on my nerves as it might. And, besides, you could not put me in any other without attracting fatal attention—anything is preferable to *that*.'

' No, not *anything*,' answered Sir William, ' not *anything*. Your care is my sacred duty, I have made it so, and I must bow to the consequences of my act, come what will. If my reputation be blasted in my old age, and men over whom I have set myself all my life as a moral censor discover at last that Sir William Temple is no better than his neighbours, and much worse than many of them, why, so be it. I will not escape by taking another step in infamy. It is my fault that you are what you are. Heaven helping me, you shall never be any worse if care can prevent it.'

Jonathan dreamily thought the ivory gates and golden had been very widely opened, and fancied Hestor smiled one of her sweet incomprehensible smiles before she answered.

'And yet I am not so dreadful but that you would be sorry to lose me.'

'Child!'

'Nay, I mean it; for I do not think you would love me so, if I were other than I am. Do not risk discovery for my sake, remember I would suffer too; perhaps you think I ought to do some work now that I am grown up, so that people may not wonder. Yes?'

'No, child, no, that would be worse and worse. No, no; I have been in the wrong to let you live here year after year and forget what might be. Something else must be arranged. By the way, have you seen young St. John? I suppose not?'

'Yes; why?'

'Nothing, I wondered.' But he drew his hand wearily across his brow and sighed. 'The Manor Cottage used to belong to his uncle. It reminded me of him. Would you object to live at the Manor Cottage?'

'I!—oh, no. But I am very happy here, much happier here. There need be no change yet, need there?' she pleaded.

She spoke in low tones, scarcely above a whisper, but with an earnestness there was no mistaking. As Jonathan heard the words, a vague doubt about whether he dreamed or not came over him. He opened his eyes, and then recollection came back like a flood. The voices again; he listened.

'That you are your own mistress is the hardest part of your fate. I cannot command——'

'Oh, don't say that, please don't. I could not bear you should doubt me so.

If you wish it, even only as a preference, I will do it, of course. It seemed a little hard just at first to go away from you and Moor Park, that was all.'

The voice trembled perceptibly. It was real beyond all doubt. Jonathan was dreaming the dream of life. Amazed beyond expression, he hesitated what to do. To discover himself would be probably to complicate matters. He had heard unwittingly what was not intended for any human ear but those to which it was addressed; but that was, so far, all his own. Sir William and Hestor need never know that any mortal was aware of some great secret being shared between them. He could trust himself to be as silent as the laurel itself. Yes, it was best to remain quiet and hope they would say no more.

' It will scarcely be going away,' answered Sir William. ' The Manor Cottage is within walking distance; I shall often see you, and you can come here sometimes.'

'Who shall I live with, and what is to be understood?' with a desperate effort at calmness which Jonathan could hear in her voice as distinctly as he could have seen it, had the laurel permitted, in her trembling lip and tearful eyes.

'I have thought of that'—there was a sob—'for God's sake don't cry, child, some one might see you.' Hestor was still in an instant. 'I have thought of that. A lady (what they call a decayed gentle-woman) is to live there, and you will nominally be her companion: as a matter of fact she will be yours. Her name is Dingley, Mrs. Dingley. She is about twice your age, but is amusing and intelligent, and, I should think, an easy person to live with. Besides, she is very discreet. Will that do?'

'Don't think me ungrateful because I

cry. You are very, very kind and good to me. I know it is all for the best.'

'I believe so. Now then, away!' saying which, after looking carefully round, Sir William Temple stooped hurriedly and kissed Hester Johnson.

Jonathan put his hand to his eyes to assure himself of the fidelity of his senses; when he withdrew it, Hester had gone, and Sir William was walking rapidly away towards the house. There was no illusion, clearly, and poor Jonathan was sorry for it; why, he could not perhaps have said. So far the future author of the Yahoo character had mingled with and thought too little of vice for the worst interpretation of every human action to be the first which occurred to him. That was not yet. 'Opinion,' he said years after, 'is not so much what a man thinks as what he is.' True, as everything he said was true; but—Jonathan! Indeed, it was not any interpretation of the incident which occurred to him first, but a feeling of intense disgust to the bird with the broken wing, and it was on that he pondered as, mechanically picking up his papers, he prepared to leave the dimly-realised confessional.

A few steps, and there before him, hanging on a branch, was a cage, and in it the raven.

'Oh! yes,' cried the bird, when it saw him.

'What!' said Jonathan, taken aback, 'are you not only a devil, but a familiar?'

'Oh, yes,'—in a whisper.

'You led me there—on purpose?'

'Oh, yes,'—louder.

'You know why?'

'Oh, yes,'—louder still.

'Shall I ever know?'

'Oh, yes—oh, yes—oh, yes!' screamed the bird, its eyes red with anger and its feathers ruffled, but sitting perfectly still.

'This is childish of me,' Jonathan tried
to say, as he strode away; but an intui-
tion told him that the raven was right—
at least, as regarded the future.

CHAPTER XV.

MATTHEW PRIOR, the subject of the late conversation between St. John and Sir William, and whose talents and misfortunes had so highly excited the admiration and sympathy of the former, was living at this time at the village of Merton, having arrived there a few days subsequently to Jonathan's departure for Moor Park. Dear Matt, as Jonathan learned one day to call him, was the son of a butcher who had lived nobody knew how and died nobody cared where. At any rate, from an age so early that he had no previous recollections, Matthew was the care of an uncle who carried on trade as a publican in Cheapside, and who did his duty by his helpless nephew in a way which very few publicans, or anybody else, have done in like circumstances. For, if 'true religion and undefiled' be to visit the widow and the fatherless in their affliction, certainly, to judge by experience, the gate *is* straight and the way *is* narrow.

Thanks to the judicious care of this humane man, Matthew found himself at fifteen years of age with just such an education as every boy similarly circumstanced ought to have, namely, enough book learning to enable him to acquire more if he chose, and an honest, manly wish and intention to work for his own living. If that was the education school-boards gave, I would not hate them as unutterably as I do. *Their* system is to tax cold mutton to supply paupers with truffles. Confiscation, sir—sheer robbery. It is a duty on which the State may insist to supply everyone with both mental and material necessities, but an impost to raise funds for teaching wastrels philology is a wicked thing directed to an idiotic object.

Matthew's uncle was a poor man, although the house over which he presided was a well-known one, and did year by year an increasing business. Well aware of this, the high-spirited orphan donned a livery the moment he could obtain permission to do so, earned a day's wages on the same terms as other servants, and insisted on his uncle accepting so-and-so much of it on account of board and lodging. For six or seven years he drudged indefatigably at this distasteful work, solacing it by the devotion of every spare moment to the study of his passion —poetry. And so, very possibly, he might have gone on many years more until his uncle dropped into the grave and left him, like Ben Jonson, free to shoulder a pike as a preferable evil to the drawing of corks. One day, however, came the incident which St. John recounted to Sir William Temple, and it altered all the course of Matthew Prior's life.

' You cannot stay in London any longer,' said his uncle to him after the rencounter; ' your chivalry, as you call it, and your rhymes will ruin us both, if you do. Why, my boy, I don't blame you so far: time was when a pretty face made a lion of me too. That is natural. There *is* something calculated to—to—what do you call it?— ferocity in a very pretty face, especially when they cry. It may not be your fault; I don't say it is, but it will never do for a tavern, *never*. Do you suppose customers expect to be knocked down because they aren't chivalrous? Nonsense, lad; there isn't such a thing as chivalrous money. Mind, I'm very glad you did it, *very*. It warmed me up to see you. Besides, you can hit out wonderfully straight. But it's not business, it doesn't pay; in fact, it means ruin. One or two may be too ashamed of getting knocked down by a waiter to tell their friends, but somebody will sooner or later, and then the friends won't come. Besides, you talked rhyme when you did it, or at least I'm sure it began with capitals, and, instead of swearing, you talked as regularly as the gurgle of wine from a bottle. Now, Matthew, gentlemen won't stand that. If they are gentlemen who like being knocked down— I mean, if they are gentlemen who don't knock back again, they won't stand rhyme. Your—yes, that's it—blank verse, odes, couplets, invocations rile that sort worse than a good thrashing. No, no,

Matthew, this will never do. You must go to the country, and I know a good opening for you when you get there.'

Matthew protested and pleaded in vain. When St. John came to procure his services as second, and when after the fight he came back to the inn and spent more money on his dinner than any five ordinary customers, Matthew thought he had a fair ground for contending that physical force *did* sometimes pay, but he still found his uncle inexorable.

'I have a family of girls, lad, and can't leave them penniless, and I am afraid they would be left so if it depended on there being two men who saw a thrashing in the same light as Mr. St. John.'

So it was settled that Matthew should go to take charge of the little inn at Merton till he sobered down his chivalry, when he should come back and relieve his uncle of most of the hard work and worry of the Cheapside business. There, then, without further preface we can follow him and watch how his efforts after the common-place affected the destinies of Jonathan Swift.

A very few days elapsed before the new landlord of the 'Cricket' was the most popular man in Merton. Everybody agreed that it was not in the nature of songs to be better sung than he sang them, or of stories to be better told than as he told them. Such songs and such stories too! How the village had got on before they had been sung and heard nobody could conceive. What insensate blindness to have been contented with 'The Harvest Home, Tol de rol,' or the story of John Lawson's ghost. It was not to be explained. So Matthew had satisfactory returns to transmit of the tavern takings;

for of course the company was gratis, the beer was not. He had plenty of time too on his hands, for the villagers plodded along very soberly all day and only became jovial in the evening. The ' rhymes, blank verse, odes, and invocations,' therefore, found a fruitful soil, and were more assiduously cultivated than ever, but, for some time after his arrival, Matthew thought that his uncle could scarcely have picked out a place better calculated to extinguish, if not respect for the fair sex, at least admiration for it.

' Ah,' he thought, ' there is not one woman in Merton whom I shall have the face to call Dorinda. Augusta isn't here, so obviously isn't here, that all the poetic license in the world won't warrant me in saying that she is. Chloe! heaven help me, not one of these people would serve for Chloe's cook.' And then he scribbled an epigram on the poor dears.

‘ Oh, Cupid, Cupid, list my sigh,
    And cure my aching smart ;
Oh, thrust an arrow in my eye
    As well as in my heart.
To Chloe, Nelly, Joan, Nannette
    I would not be unkind,
I would not—but, oh, Cupid, yet
    I must ! or else be blind !’

One morning, as he stood at the door of the ‘ Cricket,’ pondering in this frame of mind, the mathematico-philosophical question of how ugly any combination of two eyes, a nose, a chin, etcetera *could*, be made, Lauriel Swift, armed with her market-basket, marched past him.

‘ Well, I don’t know,’ he murmured, in the first blush of delighted admiration, ‘ but I am strongly of opinion that no-thing could be ugly enough to be the antithesis of *that.*’ Lauriel stopped at his neighbour the butcher’s for a minute or two, and then wended her way down the straggling High Street towards the market-place. Scarcely had she turned her back, before Matthew assailed the worthy slayer of oxen with a perfect hurricane of questions, beginning with, 'Is she human or divine?' and ending with, 'Is there any being so degraded as not to worship her?'

'Why, Mr. Prior,' said the honest man, when want of breath imposed a moment-ary cessation on that gentleman's en-comiums, 'I don't wonder at you. I should say as much myself, if I had had a London education. As it is, I am not up to the fal de rol business, the chorus like, but I think her just as pretty as you do. And she's as good as she is pretty——'

'What is she so happy about?' broke in Prior.

'Happy! I don't think she is that, poor child; she was so quiet to-day. I never remember her so quiet. Generally, she laughs and chats enough to cheer me up for the week, till she come again. But to-day she spoke so softly, I could hardly hear what she said, and her laugh was like the ripple a feather makes falling in the water.'

'Poh! that is nothing. Did you see her eyes?'

'Oh no,' replied the abashed butcher. 'Oh, dear no, I never dare look at her eyes.'

'Why?' asked Prior, in amazement.

'Because, if I did, I should ask her to marry me, and drown myself, if she wouldn't, and'—bitterly—'of course she wouldn't.'

'Come now,' said kind-hearted Prior, 'she might certainly go further and fare a great deal worse.'

'No, no, not at all. Miss Swift is a lady born. They are poor enough now, in all conscience, poorer than most people about here; but it is only the money that they have lost of their gentility.'

'She didn't look proud,' remarked Prior.

'And she does not behave as though she were; nobody less. But I know what she thinks.'

'Well, Pringle'—the butcher's name, by the way—'I'll go home and write her an ode, and since you are evidently badly hit, I'll write you one too. And, to be quite fair, you shall have your choice of which you like to send her. I won't take any mean advantages, but I intend to marry Miss Swift—wasn't it? What's her Christian name?—myself, if I can.'

'Sir,' said Pringle, turning round to him, with solemn emphasis, 'something tells me that that girl will never marry anybody.'

'Fiddlesticks, man,' retorted his lively friend, 'much love has made you mad.'

But he could extort nothing more satisfactory from the butcher than, 'I hope so, I'm sure,' and seeing that the subject was scarcely one about which the worthy man cared to converse, Prior rushed off to more willing sources of information, and readily obtained all the details which Merton could supply about the Swift family in general, and Lauriel in particular. That exhausted, he went back to the 'Cricket' and found his lieutenant, a sturdy village clod-pole, amazed and despairing.

'The gentleman has gone out, sir, in a perfect fury,' he said, alluding to a guest who had arrived the night before, 'and says you don't treat him as a government officer ought to be treated. He wished to ask you some questions, and you are not to be found.'

'Bother the fellow! why didn't he say so?' put in Prior. 'Government officers are arrogant prigs; they think that in their case the part is equal to the whole, and grumble if they don't get the homage due to King, Lords, Commons, Convocation, Queen's Bench, and the Court of Chancery collectively. I'm going out again. Goodness knows when I shall be back; certainly not till late. If our official friend grumbles any more, tell him I wouldn't stay in to oblige the small-pox, which is an officer of a much higher government than he is, and I don't see, therefore, why I should to oblige *him*.'

Saying this, he dashed off to the great pine-wood which lay to the east of Merton, and where, secure from interruption, he could have a holiday after his own heart in honour of the morning's discovery. Reading Horace, writing amatory verses, and swinging on a branch out of sheer high spirits are enjoyable occupations enough to a young man of four and twenty; but Prior prayed heartily through them all for the shades of evening, for he had made up his mind to go, directly darkness lent him courage enough, to Mrs. Swift's, and leave a copy of impassioned classical allusions for her pretty daughter. Tired at last of waiting for the dusk to draw in, he decided on going some round-about way for the sake of the walk, and, as a natural consequence of doing so, in half an hour he fairly lost himself.

'Hm!' thought Prior, 'this romance bids fair to be mixed with rheumatism. Oh! bother, and I don't even see my way to an epigram, so many have been written already under the same circumstances. Let me see, though, 'tis a punishment because I didn't come the shortest way.

> " Inflamed that his Dorinda's charms
> Her lover thus should prize,
> Who, far from rushing to her arms,

> Approached them corkscrew-wise ;
> The god of Love arranged it so."——

Hullo, what's that? A mill-wheel!' He listened. 'Yes,' he said to himself, 'it must be. I'll go and ask my way.'

Following the sound, he made his way through the wood, which every moment became more and more dense, and in places scarcely penetrable. Suddenly he stopped short. Ten paces from him on the other side of a clump of brushwood sat Lauriel Swift, and by her side was— so it at once occurred to Prior—the reason why she looked so happy. She was laughing to him a soft, rapturous little laugh that sounded, between the pulses of the torrent beside which they sat, like Paradise between chaos and the fall. Prior watched them just one moment; long enough to see that the gentleman by Lauriel's side was a handsome, soldierly man of rather foreign appearance, and then, very much disgusted to find his odes were clearly too late, he turned round and started off again for Merton.

CHAPTER XVI.

Jonathan was heartily glad to have his pitiless questionings silenced, not many minutes after we left him, by the cheery society of Henry St. John.

'Why, my dear sir,' cried that volatile gentleman, 'where on earth, if it was on earth, have you been? I thought you were lost in the essay on ancient and modern learning hunting for an original idea. Come and talk to me, do, and your petitioner will ever humbly pray. I shall not worry you long, for I leave to-morrow for London.'

'Believe me,' said Jonathan, 'I'm sincerely sorry to hear it; I had hoped your visit might be a long one. Moor Park is rather dull sometimes. Beyond Miss Johnson, there is no one with whom I can—in the proper sense of the word—converse.'

'Ah!' said St. John, 'a little wit goes a long way with a woman. It is like a parrot's talking. Perhaps it can only say five words, but one is surprised to hear it repeat at all.'

Chatting gaily thus, St. John found means ingeniously to lead the conversation to personal topics, when at once he plunged into a detailed account of who he was, where he came from, what he had done, and what he hoped to do, in short, a condensed biography, trusting thereby to extract as much in return from Jonathan. Nor was he disappointed. It is one of the few truisms that are true, that sorrow is halved and joy doubled by being shared with another; and, reserved though Jonathan had all his life been, he felt instinctively that in St. John he had found a friend in whose sympathy and discretion he could trust, and for whom he might break down something of the otherwise impenetrable barrier of his pride. Still the narrative he told was far from being a complete one, and but for the acuteness of his hearer, who read very well between the lines, it would have conveyed a most erroneous impression.

'Ah!' said St. John, breaking in at one point of the account, when he fancied Jonathan would be glad of a moment's pause to steady his voice which trembled a little with emotion, 'ah, you were educated at Dublin University.'

'Yes,' said Jonathan, 'but I fear she got but little credit by me. At that time my father was alive, and there was no probability of my having to embrace any profession for the sake of earning a livelihood. My poor father's means were not supposed to be great, but nobody, not even himself, suspected that for some years past he had been a pauper. So it turned out, however, to be. One morning, some hitch in the ordinary course of business forced him to make a thorough investigation of how things really stood, and the result was the discovery of ruin. Robbed on every hand for years, while he had carelessly been revelling in supposed success, the check came too late to be a warning. It was utter, hopeless, inevitable ruin my father saw staring from his books that morning, and not till that morning. Well, relying on my supposed financial independence, I had neglected studying for the sake of what I could make out of it. The degree course I despised, university honours I despised, as earned by the memory not the imagination. So I do now; but, had I known what was coming, I should nevertheless have exerted myself to obtain a creditable degree and a share of don laudation. They would have been of use as a means towards a " career." Of course immediately the crash came I left the university and we all retired to England, partly in hopes more openings would be found there for my energies, whatever those are worth, than in Ireland. A very few days after our arrival my father died, and my mother and sister were left to my charge, poor things. The question of what I should do became then more pressing than ever, for a small annuity my father had, and which his creditors very humanely left at his disposal, of course lapsed, and we '—he was going to say penniless, but checked himself—' were worse off than ever. Now you mustn't be hard on me when you hear what is coming. I know now how wrong I was, and would never do it again, trust me, never! A decent tradesman offered me fairly remunerative employment, so I have not even the excuse of saying that nothing else offered—no, in the teeth of opportunity, warning, common sense, I went to London with almost the last of my mother's guineas in my pocket, and there attempted to make a name and living by literature. At last, after having wasted months of valuable time, I went back beaten, but (fancy the insanity) not despairing. True, publishers would not see sense in my prose, nor poetry in my poetry, but the public would, I thought. I would storm where I could not find the sentries sleeping.'

'Heaven help literature if publishers are its sentries,' ejaculated St. John.

'Oh, went on Jonathan, 'they were passable individuals enough, well educated, well read——'

'Ugh!' retorted St. John, 'the vilest thing in the world is a commonplace man with a too good education. I detest classical statues in red brick. Well, I beg pardon for interrupting you.'

'I literally had made up my mind to publish, at my own expense or, no—would to God it had been so!—at the expense of my mother, some " choice pieces," as I fondly called them ; and I did! The attempt met with the success its morality deserved. Six copies were sold, perhaps forty were given away, and the rest rotted in the dungeon of the publisher. Then I came here. It was a better fate than I deserved, to have such a haven to come to.'

'That depends on the harbour dues,'

replied St. John, gravely. 'I am, believe me, very sorry indeed to hear of all the trouble you have had; and, as to the part that seems to grieve you most, don't think of it any longer as you do. At the worst, it was only, so far as you were concerned, an error of judgment as to public taste— a want of experience of popular imbecility. Come, come, cheer up. To judge of conduct by its consequences is well enough for publicans and attorneys, but it is beneath Jonathan Swift. By the way, it is beneath me too, so pray don't do me the injustice to fancy that I esteem you any the less for what you have told me. Unless I mistake very much, the reasons you had for publishing were exceedingly good ones, and the barque would have carried Cæsar's fortunes well enough but for the shallowness of the water in which it was launched.'

'Thank you, sir,' interposed Swift, 'ten times over for the compliment to me, and ten thousand times over for the sneer at the public.'

'Of course,' went on St. John, 'there are deep pools, but the difficulty is to find them, and the shoals and shallows often wreck the ship before the deep water has an opportunity of lending its assistance.'

St. John saw how sad were the recollections which crowded Jonathan's mind, and changed the subject.

'Let us make a compact to stand by one another all through life,' he said. 'The combined efforts of two men are far more effective than twice the effort of one.'

'Far more than twice twice,' said Jonathan. 'If six men of genius could be found of a mind, they could command the world. But as to our compact' (smiling), 'it would overset. 'Tis too lobsided. Jonathan Swift assisting Henry St. John

to realise his ambition, would be not un-
like sending a wherry to save somebody
from drowning who is safely in a sound
three-decker.   At the same time,' he went
on, warmly, 'in the very improbable circumstance of my ever having it in my
power to serve you, you may rely upon it,
Mr. St. John, that nothing will please me
better than to do so.'

'Well, at any rate, leave out the Mr.
Call me St. John, and I'll call you Swift.
I don't admit the lobsidedness of the alliance.   Just now may very well be balanced
by a very near future.   At any rate, I am
going to arrange it so.   Dorset shall see
your book, and if there are many things
in it as witty as the reason you assigned
last night why marriages are generally
unhappy—that young ladies spend most
of their time in making nets instead of
making cages—it will shortly be your turn
to recommend *me*.'

Generous enthusiasm! It is better to be enthusiastically wrong than soberly right.

CHAPTER XVII.

WHEN Prior reached Merton, he found the village in a state of great excitement. Definite news had come at last about the approaching royal visit. Delayed week after week until hope had almost expired in the breasts of the impatient villagers, the wished-for phenomenon of a real live king in Merton High Street was at last actually about to be realised.

' Hurrah !' shouted Prior, when he heard it, forgetting for the moment his disappointment. 'What a trade the " Cricket " will drive, and what an ode I'll write.'

It had not occurred to anybody to cheer so far; but the hint was taken, and Merton applauded vigorously and proclaimed its loyalty at intervals afterwards throughout the evening.

'Cloddy,' shouted Prior to his assistant, 'bring me a whole heap of eggs. I'm going to make some William the Deliverer.'

Cloddy brought them amazed, and watched with awe his London master, who went through the mystery of mixing ten eggs, a quart of brandy, five bottles of beer and some other messes with an anxious care, as though the whole combination were not fortuitous, and 'William the Deliverer' were not a brand new drink evolved, on the spur of the moment, for trade purposes, out of his own inner consciousness.

'Don't forget, Cloddy,' said Prior, with solemn emphasis, ' "William the Deliverer" must be drunk standing and served very hot.'

Before long the bar-parlour was filled by Merton luminaries who had always found, but especially since the new management, that no question of state could be really satisfactorily discussed except at the 'Cricket.' Prior welcomed everybody according to their respective tastes, with some flippant absurdity or solemn observation, and managed to make them all quite at home before the threshold was fairly crossed, which is a great point with a capable landlord. The last person to put in an appearance was the government official whose wrath Matthew had incurred by being out when he should have been under cross-examination. The man had only the air of a constable, barring the addition of being a constable out of humour. Prior had not the remotest notion who he was, but thought it wise to address him as sergeant, and then, having gained one step, to congratulate him on *not having disclosed the news.* The victory was won, and in perfect accord the bar parliament commenced its session.

(I beg pardon here for my temerity in having translated the following conversation out of its original provincialism into ordinary English. My excuse is that I am not such an unutterable idiot as to do anything else. When the original manuscript of 'Othello' is found, and it is discovered that Shakespeare put as many marginal notes as there was room for, to say 'Othello was black, Othello was black, Othello was black,' I will re-translate all the passages in this biography which require it, and take care that so important an element of character and history as is implied in a Yorkshire farmer pronouncing property 'proputty' shall not be omitted.)

'Do you really think the news is true

this time, Mr. Sergeant,' demanded Prior of that gentleman, 'or are we to be disappointed again? Ah! I see, you are afraid of letting out too much if you say anything. Come, Mr. Smith, tell the sergeant what the information positively is, and then he will know just how much the authorities have thought fit to tell us. Just one minute first, though. Cloddy,' (calling), 'bring some " William the Deliverer." I think, gentlemen, that, under the circumstances, we can't do less than have a glass of the generous liquor which bears the name of our king. And it might be proper, gentlemen, to drink it standing with three times three.' The proposal being carried, and carried out, 'Now then, Mr. Smith, your humble servants.'

'Well,' said the individual thus addressed, 'the letter isn't exactly official, but they say that no official notice is going to be given anywhere, for fear it should be said that the king's reception was got up by the Court. It is only a hint, after all, you know; black ink, common paper —I saw it myself—and no seal. It seems a pity not to put a seal.'

'Oh,' put in a well-to-do farmer, 'the great seal has never been used since the warrant to murder the royal martyr was stamped with it, no doubt that's why.'

'No doubt,' chimed everybody, and then Mr. Smith went on to tell of what the letter contained, from which it appeared that the king was coming in three days' time, that he would spend a few minutes in Merton while changing horses, and would then go straight on. It was trusted that the loyal inhabitants of Merton would not be too lavish in adorning the town for the occasion, as the king would be sorry to feel that his visit had caused the least inconvenience to any of his subjects.

'I think you may be quite sure it is true this time,' put in the sergeant, 'quite sure.'

'Bravo!' cried Prior. 'Here, gentlemen, the king! the king of Merton!'

'Now,' said Mr. Smith, when the toast had been duly honoured, 'what are we to do? How is His Majesty to be received? I protest against Merton being lumped in with the county. *We* must receive him ourselves. The place may be small, but it isn't unimportant.'

'Certainly not,' cried Prior, 'there are a great many counties in England, but there is only one Merton.'

So it was carried, amid shouts of approval, that Merton was to distinguish itself in a unique and original manner quite distinct from the county rejoicings.

'But,' said Mr. Smith, in a moment of inspiration, when this point had been decided, and everybody—for Matthew made a point of not appearing more wise than his customers in any way they could understand—seemed of opinion no lions were left in the way; 'it's all very well to say we will do something, but what?'

'We can put on our best and cheer,' said somebody.

But everybody saw the fallacy of that. There would be a want of distinctiveness about it. All the county would do no less. It was long before light was seen through the difficulty. At length some one suggested a presentation of home manufacture. 'Merton ale!' was the unanimous and instantaneous reply from all the luminaries. Fancy having forgotten Merton ale! Why, King Charles II. would touch nothing else, when he drank beer at all. Now we've got it. The king shall have a cask of ale, the very best brewed.

'Cloddy,' shouted Prior, 'bring some Merton ale—the best. The king, gentlemen, the king!'

And in a thorough good humour with themselves and all men, they honoured His Illustrious Majesty for the seventeenth time. The host saw that his guests' good temper was such that he might venture on making a suggestion to their collective wisdom.

'We might even do more,' he said. 'Let us give him a pottery-ware flagon, such as our friend Jenkyns there makes, with a draught of beer in it just ready to drink. He can't be expected to tap the cask on the spot, can he? And yet I shouldn't wonder if he did, when he has finished the flagon. Have some more of your brother-in-arms, "William the Deliverer," Mr. Sergeant. And then, you know, as to who is to present it, let us get all the prettiest girls in Merton, dressed in white, hair down their backs, flowers—— Heaven—and the prettiest of the prettiest shall march at their head, and give Solomon Alexander, our beneficent monarch, the flagon on her bended knee, while the others, like a halo——'

He never got any further, the applause drowned him.

'Well, gentlemen,' said the sergeant, when the noise subsided, ' I'm surprised, I confess, to see so many of you alive and well, because if you agree about which is the prettiest girl in Merton I should have fancied a good few would have black eyes to show for it. If you don't, how are you going to settle?'

Five seconds later it was quite clear they did *not* agree, and that there was no chance of their doing so this side the grave. Polly, Peg, and Poppetty, Mary Ann, Susan, and a dozen others had each fervant and unflinching supporters. It seemed that the sergeant was going to prove in the right. Expressions were rapidly becoming unparliamentary, and the meeting threatened to break up in disorder.

'Stay, gentleman,' said Prior, when he thought the discord had become sufficiently pronounced to inculcate the impossibility of any other solution, 'let us cast lots who shall nominate the goddess,' and, no one objecting, he put in the crown of a hat a certain number of blank pieces of paper, and, as his friends supposed, another, which was marked with the fatal sign. This last, however, for the honour of Merton taste and various other reasons, he thought better to reserve to himself, so as to make sure of drawing it, and the harmless chicane succeeding admirably, he called upon the company to rise while he gave as his toast and divinity 'Stephanie Swift.'

'Bless you,' shouted honest Pringle, who so far had been conspicuous for his silence, 'Miss Swift ! ! ! If she gives the king his flagon and makes an exhibition of herself my name's not Pringle. She's too good for the job. Choose another. You're wasting your time.'

Prior, however, was firm. 'He would,' he said, 'write an ode, in the name of Merton, begging her to undertake the task, and if she refused the voice of the muses, why—but she won't, she can't. It shall begin thus :

"Come, Stephanie, come——" '

'That won't do,' persisted Pringle, 'the family call her Lauriel now, they've dropped Stephanie, and, besides, what right have you to speak to her like that?'

'Poetic license,' laughed Prior. 'Well, gentlemen, may I try?'

The guests were getting sleepy by this time : leave was accorded with only Pringle as a dissentient voice, and the members went home to bed. Matthew was delighted with his success, and not at all in the humour to follow his guests, so he induced Mr. Sergeant to sit up a little longer and have a final chat. William III. was a notoriously reserved man, but the caricature namesake of him Prior had concocted was very opposite in its tendencies. Distinctly influenced by his royal master, Mr. Sergeant presently shook Prior warmly by the hand and remarked to him that 'he was sure nobody could better keep a secret.'

'I'm sure I'm very sorry,' answered the lord of the 'Cricket.' 'It is a failing of mine to be reserved and disagreeable; however, I hope you won't mind it. Everybody has his faults.'

'On the contrary,' went on the magnanimous officer, enflamed by something of his attributed profession, 'it has inspired my confidence. I love you for it, sir, even more than for your wit. Is there any fear of being disturbed? Mum's the word.'

'Not the least.'

'Well, then, I'll tell you straight out, and trust to your honour to give me information if you can; that's ten times better than cross-examination with a gentleman of your stamp. I am down here on very special business. Information has been received that a French spy has been seen about here, a fellow called Guiscard— some time ago, you know; he may not be here now. But the question is what he ever wanted here. Why, nobody ever knew him anywhere but what the object was devilry, more or less.' Prior's attention was aroused, and the officer saw it. 'Have you seen him?' he asked. 'Recognise the description, eh?'

'Well, it isn't very distinctive as yet,'

answered the poet. 'It suits everybody but you and me. Is there nothing more unusual about him than a taste for devilry? What colour is his hair? Does he squint? Do his toes turn in?'

The sergeant fumbled in his pocket and drew out a paper of instructions, while Prior mixed vigorously at the jug of 'William the Deliverer.' He felt convinced that the description about to be read would tally with the individual he had seen a few hours before at the waterfall, and feared the premonition might, in that case, not save him from betraying some emotion. The sergeant stumbled through his instructions, description and all, and Prior's doubt became certainty. Afraid of being questioned, he dropped the weapon with which he was lashing the imperturbable liquor into a frenzy, shook his new-found friend warmly by the hand, regretted that he could not (in the sense of did not choose) give him any information, but felt honoured by having one whom the government trusted with so important a commission beneath his roof.

'One more glass, and then perhaps we had better go to bed.'

For Prior had really taken a fancy to Lauriel Swift, and felt vaguely uneasy at the turn affairs were taking.

'Possibly to-morrow,' he thought, 'I shall see my way to getting more information at less risk.'

CHAPTER XVIII.

THE following evening Monsieur de Guiscard paid a short visit to Vane Castle to explain to its honourable master the arrangement he had made for the execution of their great scheme. After deploring that the short notice given of the precise date would render the execution less certain than it would otherwise have been, he went on to explain the following design to his lordship, and entreat assistance :

'I would not have been so long,' he said, 'in stating definitely my plans, and availing myself of your advice in perfecting them, had I not been in daily expectation of receiving valuable information from my agent—the only agent I have got in England—and which, as it might have changed the whole tenor of our enterprise, I thought it well to wait for before troubling you with the details of a perhaps to be abandoned project. I am the more sorry for this now, as, after all, the fellow has procured me but little really valuable information or anything else; and considering his position as private secretary to Sir William Temple, where all the private dispatches from the usurper must come into his power, if he please, and remembering that on every question of the slightest importance Sir William is consulted, it is too bad that it should be so. I had quite reason, surely, for anticipating something of consequence should be communicated which should facilitate matters. Of course, a mere shot with a blunderbuss can be arranged in two minutes; but I confess I was anxious not to be so clumsy as that in the affair. The age demands a more finished assassination'—smiling—'a bell-pull assassination. However, as I say——'

'Who is Sir William's secretary?' put in Lord Vane.

'Oh, I must tell you about that. Before I had been twenty-four hours in my present hiding-place, I discovered that the son of my hostess, a clever, intelligent fellow, was a rank Jacobite, as all clever, intelligent fellows are—a very rank Jacobite indeed. I drew out his opinions as well as I could, without exposing my own, and presently learnt that the great object of his ambition was to be instrumental in wreaking the vengeance of his rightful king upon the tyrant. After this we talked long and earnestly about the unhappy state of the country, and at length I felt justified in admitting him to my confidence in so far as was necessary to procure his co-operation.'

'But what good could he do you?' asked Lord Vane.

'Why, this,' was the answer. 'His mother is related in some dim, distant, undiscoverable way to Sir William, and so he sometimes does the family a good turn when he can. Well, he chanced to have no secretary, and Jonathan Swift chanced to be very hard put to for something to eat at the same time. So Sir William offered the post to the young man. Do you see?'

Lord Vane nodding his assent, De Guiscard went on—

'It may have been bad luck, but it certainly looks wonderfully like bad management, that a whole month of free leave to pry about Moor Park should have produced so little result. At any rate, the broad fact is, that nothing has come of it. And now—— ?'

' I find,' said the other, ' that there has throughout been a fallacy in my original argument. This distresses me very much, for certainly, with so short a time remaining in which to make the necessary arrangements, and deprived, as this must deprive you, of the mainstay of your hopes, to desert you seems very like deserting you to the power of certain failure. Consider now, can you help me out of it? We agreed that it was quite *justifiable* to kill a tyrant; but is it *always* wise to do so ; and, if not, is it so in this case? I think not; because such is the constitutional delicacy of the Prince of Orange that he cannot possibly live many years longer, and his continued existence for, say, sixty months is a lesser evil than would be the sympathy engendered by his assassination.'

The reader will please remember that this was in the year 1695, and that professorial or Germanic politics had not been expounded as they have more recently been by the parliamentary representatives of various populous, if not intellectual, districts. So, although Monsieur de Guiscard had all along expected some turn of the sort, he was heartily astonished when he heard it. Making the best of the situation, he presently drew a long breath and sadly shook his head.

'I'm afraid, my lord, your argument is right,' and then, after a pause—'But surely the fact is not as you imagine?'

From this resulted a long discussion on the *merits of the case*, that being the *last* step with Lord Vane, as it nowadays is with so many. De Guiscard supported his view with all the warmth necessary to be beaten with credit, and then, surrendering to the pressure of irresistible logic, he abjured the enterprise in a voice which trembled with emotion.

'How exceedingly fortunate,' he thought, as he wended his way to the cottage a little later, 'that the fellow should so readily have helped me out of the scrape of his association. That is an end,' he said to himself. But no, it was in one sense only a beginning. Little did he imagine what fruit would be borne by that luxuriant lie at the expense of Sir William Temple's secretary.

He was met at the door of the cottage by Lauriel, who held out to him, with a laughing face, a long copy of verses inscribed on parchment. The fear that her lover should be discovered had been gradually dulled by his long immunity; and his evening solitary walks had ceased to terrify by the apprehension of what they might entail. Thus Lauriel's life had come to be, even in its hardships and deprivations, all sunshine and laughter, which beamed and rippled everywhere; so that sometimes her brother wondered at the brightness of her letters, and was troubled at the clearness of the golden note.

'What is that, my own?' he asked, taking the paper. 'What! verses; nay, I shall be jealous. That will never do.'

'Well, I'm sure you needn't. *Imprimis*, as Jonathan says, because they are a good deal more about Venus than about me; and secondly, because I don't like them. Now, fancy! what would Jonathan say, if Stephanie Swift, Lauriel in inverted commas, should go to Merton on a public occasion to hand about beer!'

'They want improving,' remarked the count, referring to the verses, 'with which view, I should esteem it a great favour if you would read them to me. I have read the prose.'

While she read, in a soft, melodious voice, as follows, Monsieur de Guiscard sat, with his head resting on his hand, thanking his stars for the most marvellous piece of good fortune that ever befell a conspirator.

> ' " I've watched the ocean swell, my sweet,
>   And shuddered at its roar;
>   Yet it but cast one shell, my sweet,
>   That tide upon the shore.

> ' " I've heard the north wind blow, my sweet,
>   In all its mighty power;
>   'Twas but to shake the snow, my sweet,
>   From our poor shivering flower." '

And so on to the realms of ancient mythology.

Having finished which, she said, with emphasis,

' Being interpreted in the light of the " prose," this means, will you come and hand the king a glass of beer in the name, and as representing, seventeen cobblers and a publican's apprentice. Should

you have thought there was such im-
pudence in the great city of Merton?'

'It is very terrible, is it not?' he answered, looking up with a smile.

'As terrible as a gratuitous insult to
polite poverty can be,' she replied, a little
hurt at the count's apparent indifference.
'It is equivalent to saying, there is nothing in your manners, bearing, intelligence, &c., &c., to discriminate you from
a farm labourer, therefore you may as
well represent one for the occasion.'

The count was silent.

'Don't think me proud and disagreeable,' she went on, 'but it is hard to be
confounded with those whom one *knows*
are one's inferiors merely for lack of a
few wretched guineas.'

'It was not that, pretty one,' he said,
with lifelike sadness. 'How could I think
you proud or disagreeable. I was silent
because I was going to ask you some-

thing which, from what you say, I fear you will think it cruelty to ask, and yet——'

All Lauriel's dormant fears were aroused in an instant.

'Oh, Henri! is there news? Is there more danger? Have you been seen?'

'No, darling; it is not that, nothing to do with that, except indeed thus far, that so it may be any moment, until I am either pardoned or—dead.' And then, with an assumption of assumed gaiety, as perfect of its sort as the preceding melancholy had been, "Something much worse than that. Guess again.'

But she only shook her pretty little head wonderingly. He rose and took her hand.

'Lauriel, I will tell you, because I believe you love me, really love me, and, if you do, I know you would be only too ready to do what, my pretty one, I wish you should. You can save me, Lauriel. This opportunity is one that may never recur, never. Is it selfish that I ask you to grasp it while you can?'

'What is it, Henri?' she answered. 'I will do for you all and more than all that I would do for myself or even for my mother or Jonathan. Don't distrust me, please don't,' and her innocent, pleading eyes looked full into his as though there were no such thing in the world as treachery, or in love as disappointment.

'I do not deserve such love, my Lauriel,' he answered. 'You are an angel, darling. Come,' he continued, 'after all, though you will think my request but little short of martyrdom, it is really not so very dreadful. For, whether you succeed or not, we shall not stay here much longer. Lauriel, I want you to do as these Merton people wish. Present the flagon to the king, and *present along with it a petition for justice to poor Henri de Guiscard.*'

Lauriel looked at her lover for a moment with great eyes, in which wonder predominated; then a laugh overpowered the wonder, and she fairly clapped her hands with delight.

'Oh, how stupid of me not to have thought of that before. Fancy supposing I should object to that. I'm going upstairs to tell mamma. What a pity Jonathan isn't here to write the petition.'

CHAPTER XIX.

'Sir William begs, sir, that you will go to him at your convenience, he is in the west garden,' said a servant to Jonathan on the afternoon of the same day on which occurred the events recorded in the last chapter.

Jonathan went forthwith, wondering at the unusual summons. He had never, except on the occasion of the dinner, uttered five words to the great man outside the study. To be spoken to in the west garden was a novelty. Late events, however, had dulled the edge of the marvellous.

Jonathan was quite prepared for the unexpected to happen.

Sir William, when Jonathan approached,
was superintending with keen anxiety some
surgical operations upon a rose, by which
whig politics were mingled with horticul-
ture in the proportion of ten to one, and
Nature, in that ratio, sacrificed to reminis-
cences of the Hague.

'Pardon me,' he said, 'one moment.
These fellows will make some mistake or
other if I relax my vigilance for the twink-
ling of an eye. Their idea of a straight
line is—there, thank goodness, that will
do.' (To the men.) 'You will please leave
it exactly as it is till my return. Now, Mr.
Swift, I am at your service, what I wished
to see you about is a matter of some importance. Will you give me your arm?
Thank you. The fact is that I sat up all
last night writing a dispatch, and at my
years that is hard work. This morning

just retribution makes me feel very shaky. However, that will wear off in the air sooner than indoors.'

Jonathan Swift, linked arm in arm with Sir William Temple, furtively rubbed his eyes with the disengaged hand. No, he was not dreaming: then he stole a glance at his patron. Was *he?* Certainly not. Nobody was ever more perfectly wide awake than the ex-ambassador. Astonished though Jonathan was at the extraordinary change of tone in Sir William's conduct to him, it after all admitted of a very easy explanation. No two natures could be more diverse than were those of the secretary and the statesman. The one was a type and the other an individual. Sir William certainly was a very estimable, intelligent type of a very estimable, intelligent class, but Jonathan Swift——'

'Nature broke the mould in which she cast him.'

So, having no more appreciation of the genius of his secretary than a deaf man has of an oratorio, and further, having begun with a violent prejudice against him, it had never occurred to Sir William that Jonathan Swift might have the ordinary talents of a clever man as well as his own individual inspiration.

The encomiums of Henry St. John had astonished him, and made him *look*, which, after all, is the first step towards seeing, and the step the omission of which is the fertile cause of most of the ignorance, bigotry, freethinking, and humbug with which this world is so plentifully stocked. Directly he looked he saw. Jonathan's discussion of the Triennial Bill convinced him that St. John was right. Having discovered thus much, various circumstances in the work of the last month recurred to him, all confirmatory of his new opinion, whereupon Sir William, who was not wanting in decision of character, came at once to the conclusion that his secretary might be usefully employed on higher class work than he had hitherto been trusted with, and that he deserved to be put on an altogether different footing.

This being so, Sir William proceeded to treat Jonathan Swift as a confidential political assistant. .He was quite conscious that Jonathan might be surprised at the sudden change from the buttery to the walk he was then enjoying, but that was of no consequence whatever, and called for no explanation, however hinted. He had treated the young man as society ordained a gentleman should treat a superior servant, whether that servant knew Greek or not; but, having promoted him to be the really confidential secretary of a statesman, his future treatment would correspond with his new position.

'A dispatch from the king came yester-

day, as you know,' began Sir William.
' The Triennial Bill about which you talked
so ably last night '—Jonathan made a
gawky inflection—' is the leading question of the hour. Shrewsbury showed
himself greatly deficient in common sense
in introducing it—of that there is no
question. The sad results of its previous
agitation were long felt—indeed, we may
safely say they are felt still in the turmoil
of the political world. However, the bill
is to be introduced ; the peers will pass it
unanimously, and then, what is the king
to do? Should he reject it again on his
own responsibility, firstly for his country's
good, and secondly for his own, or should
he not? His majesty wishes to run the
risk of throwing it out. My opinion is
that to do so would be madness. The new
parliament would be disgusted at the out-
set, and then heaven knows how it may
all end. Well, the Duke of Portland is

coming to see what I think about it, though in all conscience there can be very little doubt about my opinions now, surely, and then he is going to inform the king. This won't do. Portland is a soldier; I am too ill to go myself, and a dispatch is almost useless. Such things must be talked over, and ably talked over, to effect any useful purpose; so, Mr. Swift, I am afraid I must ask you to go for me and see what *you* can do.'

Jonathan again bowed.

' I shall be very glad to do everything in my power,' he said, 'and shall exert myself to ensure as satisfactory a result as may be practicable.'

He felt that he ought to profess the gratitude which he certainly felt for this opportunity for distinction and the confidence implied in it, but he could not bend his haughty spirit so low. There was nothing in what Sir William was doing but a commercial appreciation of a vendible commodity. He had found out his secretary could run a certain errand, so he bade him run; and Jonathan, smarting under the neglectful insults of a month which had seemed a century, could not find it in his heart to say, 'Thank you.'

'Thanks for this,' he thought, 'would imply that my month upon the rack was all to which my desert entitled me.'

Sir William probably understood this. At any rate there was no alteration of tone or manner to evince displeasure, and after affably explaining every point of importance, including details of Court etiquette, he concluded by saying,

'As to the dispatch, I leave that to you. The king will probably never read it; all he will do will be to listen more or less attentively to what you have to say when you have to hand it to him. By the way, of course, you know that His Majesty is at Lincoln, unless he has already left for Derbyshire. I wish that procession were well over,' he muttered, parenthetically. 'Your trip, therefore, will not be a London outing. You will have to catch him just where he happens to be. The route is sketched in this letter of the Duke of Portland's; let me see—yes, there it is; but remember, as yet it is strictly secret! It does not do in these times to give too much notice of His Majesty's whereabouts.'

The conference over, Jonathan returned to the house, and, meeting St. John at the door, he told him with sparkling eyes of his good fortune.

'You have been so kind as to applaud me to Sir William—I am sure of it,' he said. 'This has not come about in the natural course. I won't thank you for it —not a word—I will do more. I will never attempt to discharge the obligation.

It shall be a pleasure to me to be in your
debt.'

And St. John, seeing the nature of the
man with whom he had to deal, looked
upon that as a very high compliment
indeed.

Next morning early Jonathan started
on his embassy, having St. John for a
travelling companion as far as London.

'Thank goodness,' cried Jonathan, when
they were fairly off, 'that the cross country roads are all abominable. Could I
have got at Lincoln more directly, I should
have missed your company. As it is, I
am perfectly happy.'

'So am I,' answered St. John, 'subject
only to a regret that you are in such a
violent hurry. If you could spare four
hours at most in London, I *might* be able
to come north with you. The uncle of
my friend Prior had a little tavern in
Derbyshire left him by a distant relative

some time ago, and there was some idea
of Prior being deputed to look after it.
If I find he has gone, I shall take a trip
down to see him. Four hours would
suffice for all my business in London.
What do you say?'

'I say it is an unmitigated nuisance.
Four minutes is more than I can afford.
Can't you manage in four minutes?
Derbyshire, too! You could have come
to Lincoln, and then gone back with me
to Derbyshire. Sir William kindly agreed
to my coming back round that way to
visit my mother, who lives near a little
place called Merton in that county.'

'Merton,' said St. John—'how odd!
It is to Merton Prior has gone or is going.
Let me see, the tavern's name was—yes,
the "Cricket."'

Swift, however, protested he could not
wait. His instructions were to spare no

effort to catch the king, to whose popularity and success in what was really a gigantic personal canvass, a definite declaration on the triennial bill would, Sir William felt, be of the utmost consequence. So the young men regretfully proceeded to make the best of their present companionship.

'We shall have a grand time of it at Merton if you reach it whilst I am there,' remarked St. John. 'You and Prior would be great fun.'

'What? All that sport for one Philistine?' laughed Jonathan, to whom the merest suspicion of being exhibited was an abomination. 'No, no, we must have a triangular duel. By the way, you must have wondered why I don't ask more about Prior's work. All my questions have referred to the flesh and blood of him exclusively. The fact is that you called him a poet, and to my mind criticism of *poetry* is absurd. You can't translate a sense into language. We feel, but we cannot feel in words. We hear, but, though we hear words, we do not hear *in* words, we *see*, and there's an end of it. Now poetry is colour. You can't explain it. It appeals directly to a certain sense which some men have and some have not, and which is as distinct from any other sense, as the sense of sight is from that of hearing. No explanation will convey the faintest appreciation of colour to a blind man, and similarly no explanation will enable anybody but a poet to appreciate poetry. When I read the Shakespeare that is really Shakespeare I give utterance to what no more admits of definition or criticism than the tinting of the rainbow or the music of the spheres.'

'Right, by the prophet,' cried St. John, who had a volume of the 'Turkish Spy' in his pocket. 'I believe, after all, there *are* ten wise men in Israel who know the difference between verses full of accuracy, elegance, sentiment, pathos, thought, wit, and human kindness, and INSPIRATION. I am glad of support for my opinions, because I get it so seldom, and because I am passionately in earnest.'

'Nay,' said Jonathan, 'don't be jealous. It is a hundred to one odds that violent zeal for truth is either petulancy, ambition, or pride.'

'To the two latter of which there is but little objection,' laughed his companion.

'None whatever, unless they are ashamed of themselves, and sail under false colours. In fact, quite the contrary.'

And so, chatting merrily, London was at length reached, and the young men parted with many expressions of mutual esteem and regard.

'I shall see you soon again,' said Henry

St. John, as he turned to go, 'at the outside, three days.'

Alas those three days !

END OF THE FIRST VOLUME.

LONDON: PRINTED BY DUNCAN MACDONALD, BLENHEIM HOUSE.

9 783337 048136